The
Vice
President
DIRECTIVE
17
The Origins

Carolinadeivid

TOUCH
LADYBIRD
LUCKY
STUDIOS
A CAROLINADEIVID PRODUCTION 2018

DEDICATION

"Today's leaders have backtracked taking us back to the medieval times. The whole system has gone bonkers relying on digital-man-made-agents to function properly. We still spend $trillions globally making weapons. Sometimes war is the answer. A new beginning. Destruction of the things we don't need; weapons. Ladies and gentlemen above all, this gives me the President the chance to play God and eliminate all evil once and for all. Uphold the rule of the law. Surely you don't want to be on my *To-do-list* or you will feel the full force of Directive 17."

DISCLAIMER

This is a work of fiction. Names, characters, businesses, places, events, and incidents are either the products of the author's imagination or used in a fictitious manner. Any resemblance to actual persons, living or dead, or actual events is purely coincidental.

ACKNOWLEDGMENTS

A big thanks to Touchladybirdlucky Studios and best wish to the Carolinadeivid Brand.

CHAPTER ONE

One bright afternoon a door of one of the houses suddenly opened and a tall beautiful lady walked out toward a car parked outside a huge mansion. She stopped outside the mansion next to the car. She instantly opened the car door and stopped and looked at the top bedroom window. Instantly a man flipped open the curtain and looked on talking on the phone.

"I love you."

"I know darling."

The woman entered the car leaving the door opened.

"I have to go darling see you later."

"Karolina. I love you very much. I just don't know what I would do without you my love."

"I know darling see you soon..."

"I know that's all you have to say?"

"What do you want me to say?"

"How about I love you too?"

"Words can't come easy to some of us. It's obvious I love you too darling."

"I know but it's nice to hear the words from you."

"Can we talk when I get back?"

"Sure. I am just saying that one day you will come back and find me gone."

The woman stopped and threw a quick glance at the bedroom window.

"Where would you go?"

"I just can't understand that if I love you this much why you don't show me the same love."

"I have to go. Can we talk when I get back. I understand what you are saying darling. I just have been busy of late."

The man lowered down the hand holding the cellphone and looked through the window.

A huge white Volvo executive class car pulled out of the drive way and into the road and silently disappeared up the highway. The woman looked in the rear-view mirror before the ringing of the car phone startled her.

"Yes. Karo speaking. How can I help you?"

After a while the car turned into a side road before pulling up on the roadside outside a house. She wore her sunglasses and stood just by her car. Momentarily another elegant woman smartly dressed came out of the house.

"Right on time!" she shouted.

"Big day we can't afford to fuck up. Everything should be as smooth as planned."

"Nothing to worry about it should be okay. Karo."

Soon afterward the two women's car headed out of the suburbs.

"What's that teenager-smile on your face?"

Karolina smiled even further and threw a quick glance at Californika.

"Jonathan?"

"I don't know why he is acting like a teenager in love."

"What happened?"

"He has been very emotional lately."

There was a moment of silence. All they could hear in the background was the song; Seductive Handsome Man by Carolinadeivid.

It began on a lovely Saturday evening.

He was handsome and the most Seductive Man that night.

He was my lover to be, I knew it then and there. My Seductive handsome man. My Man.

…...

That's how it happened:

Oh yeah! Oh yeah!

I ogled a Seductive Man.

"Feeling insecure?"

"I don't think so. I think he is feeling unloved lately. Honestly, I can't blame him. I have been very busy lately. I am pushing very hard to make everything go according to plan. It's not easy you know."

"Maybe he needs some TLC's."

"He is saying that I am taking him for granted and that one day he might leave me."

Californika looked at Karolina briefly before looking outside the window.

"Leaving you? I thought you had something going on between you."

"He doesn't feel my love nowadays, and he thinks that I am lucky to have him. Just this morning he said that I am taking him for granted."

"Do men really show that kind of love? Mine can't be asked every time I raise the subject. He is like, off course I love you that's why I am still with you."

"I must confess Jonathan has been showing some real love toward me it's only that I was too busy to take notice."

The background song can be heard as silence broke out.

Last summer I kissed a seductive man

Still, he is in my thoughts.........

The car approached the city. A few minutes later it stopped outside one of the main buildings in the city. The women got out and entered the building. A lot of people were in the reception talking.

"Excited?"

"Not really. Could have been better if we owned this."

"You are never satisfied. Are you?"

"It's not that. If this new shop was mine, then I would be very happy."

"We are getting paid that's what matters to me."

"I am just saying that maybe it's time we go it alone."

Californika stopped and looked at Karolina.

"It's not easy you know. Do you know how many have failed? How many have blown away all their life-savings with no returns at all?"

"I am not all those people. I might strike it big."

"Or regret it. I think it is still early to start thinking about all that. You will need a strong partner. Someone who understand and knows about these things."

"I am looking at one right now."

Californika walked away for a while. She stopped and looked at Karolina. She smiled for a while.

"That's flattering but you know Tom is after a vacation house in Spain. This business thing is out of the question."

Instantly the lift doors suddenly opened. A man smartly dressed up in a white suit and a blue tie came out. He smiled before rubbing his hands together.

"Can I have your attention! This is the time you have been waiting for! Are you all excited?"

The people replied but not loud enough.

"Are you hungry or what?" he asked.

A huge buzz sound filled the reception.

"Follow me if you can please!"

The crowd followed him. In the building and across the reception on the other side were two big doors. A ribbon was across the doors. Karolina felt confident inside but looked a bit nervous. As soon as the regional director appeared out of the lifts, she hurried toward the door.

"Ladies and gentlemen. The regional director Mr. Karl and the head of this store Mrs. Karolina!"

A huge applause and jubilation filled the hall.

Months later.

An executive Mercedes Benz rolled out of the mansion's yard and slowly into the road. Karolina looked nervous as she looked everywhere first. The look on her face said it all. Fear. Yes, fear of some kind. The car turned into the main road and disappeared around a corner. She looked in the rear-view mirror and everywhere. She looked at the passenger seat and pulled her bag close to herself quickly looking ahead in the road. She opened the bag while focusing ahead and quickly took out a gun. She stared at the gun for a split second. She placed the gun on the passenger seat. The screeching of the car tires sends her panicking. She looked in the rear-view mirror before she sped off. The chase. She looked at the car behind her. She cursed. Fear and panic sat in. She then abruptly pressed on the brakes and stopped the car beside the road. She grabbed her gun and pushed the door open. Breathing heavily, she stared at the car coming her way. The car driver instantly harsh brakes skidding before coming to a halt just before hers. Inside was an unrecognizable Jonathan. He looked worried and heartbroken of some sort. Karolina didn't even notice how he got out of his car so fast. She only saw him coming toward her, fast with a face casting a lot of emotional pain and confusion.

"Stop there Jonathan! I have a gun!"

Jonathan walked fast toward her as if he didn't hear a

word she said.

"Jonathan! Stop there! I have a gun."

She raised the gun and aimed at Jonathan.

"That's right! It's loaded," she cocked up the gun.

That made Jonathan instantly stop for a while.

"What? Shoot me for what? I love you Karolina."

"No, you don't. We talked about this remember."

"I love you Karolina."

"Jonathan don't upset me. Don't start. You don't walk away from the people you love. Okay?"

Jonathan looked down for a split second. He touched his heart and stretched his hand.

"Come my darling. You know I used to love you."

"Exactly! Used to. I moved on you do the same. Okay?"

"I mean I love you."

"Do you really Jonathan? Search your heart do you have love for me? Do you Jonathan!"

She shouted leaning toward Jonathan.

He murmured something with a troubled face and looked at Karolina.

"I loved you with all my heart. I just don't know why I can't feel the love I had for you."

"You are heartbroken. Your heart has no love

whatsoever for me. I might start to believe that you never loved me. If you loved me, you could not have walked away from me."

"I honestly don't know what happened."

"I know! Let me help you explain. You lost your love for me. It happens Jonathan no big deal but don't come and rub it on my face. I have moved on. Move on with your life."

"Karolina! I love you. I mean I loved you."

"Oh my God! I know you told me so many times. Move on. For the good times we had please move on. You lost your love for me a long time ago. Even then when we were together. Remember threatening to walk away? Exactly what you ended up doing. No big deal. I only get upset that even now you admit you don't have love for me yet you keep on nagging me. What do you want from me Jonathan?"

Jonathan looked at Karolina and sauntered toward her. She lowered the gun and dropped it to the ground and started sobbing.

"Oh, Jonathan what is going on with you? You are confusing me now. What do you want?"

Jonathan silently hugged Karolina, and the two stood there for a while before getting into Karolina's car. The cars parked there for some time before Jonathan jumped into his car and sped off.

Months later one sunny beautiful day a lot of people

had gathered outside a huge store in the city. A large crowd had gathered outside to witness the opening of a new shop. The usher appeared as the door opened. He walked toward Karolina and poured some champagne. She took the glass and smiled before looking at the people in the crowd. She raised the glass and smiled further. Californika and Tom appeared from one corner.

"Congratulations Karo you made it. I am proud of you. I never thought you can do this on your own?"

"Thanks Cali. If it wasn't for you and my new man, there..." She looked on the other side and raised the champagne glass.

"I probably could not have made it."

"A lot of effort and money had gone into this project."

"Imagine how things turned out in the end. The separation was somehow a blessing. I ended up with a new store of my own. If I was still with Jonathan, I might not be standing here today celebrating with you my friend."

"So how is he any news?"

"Last time I saw him he was heartbroken, confused and suicidal. Even now I can't understand it. You don't walk away from love and become heartbroken yourself."

They all laughed.

"Are you sure he was not taking any drugs? That's not human behavior. What did he say about all this?"

"Stolen heart. Someone stole his love. Speaking of which...."

She looked in the other direction and saw Nick coming toward her. A handsome strong man with short yet volumized hair, dimples, a million-dollar smile and oozing charm.

"Yeah, I can see why after dumping you Jonathan now feels that someone stole his love. Where did you find this guy?"

"Jonathan is very funny. He said that someone literally stole his love for Karolina."

Quipped Californika looking at her partner before all eyes were on Nick.

"Ooh my darling. You look fabulous. I am lucky to have you. What did I do to deserve such a beautiful and successful lady, my true love?"

Californika and Tom looked at each other and nodded in admiration.

"I am proud of you darling. Not many would go through what you went through. I admire that in you. In fact, that's one of the hundred reasons why my knees melt at the thought of you. Cali and my best friend-to-be Tom. I am a one lucky guy because of this beautiful woman here."

He opened his arms and hugged Karolina before the

couple started kissing.

Instantly everyone started clapping hands and applauding. He took center stage soon afterward.

"Ladies and gentlemen, I have been to many places and met new people. All kinds of people but I have never met such a loving and ambitious lady like my lady, Karo. That first day I met her, I knew it straight away that we will be a successful couple one day and today is just the beginning. Ladies and gentlemen. Ms. Karolina. The owner of this new shop. Best wishes to us too."

He started clapping hands and the whole crowd joined in. One strong breath and the stage was hers.

"It took a lot to be here today ladies and gentlemen, but I tell you this, it was worth it. How funny life can be. I lost my love but got an even better man in Nick. A man who shares the same dreams as me. A visionary and successful businessman. My business partner and my love...."

"He stole my love! He is nothing but a thief. A love-thief if you ask me. A heart-thief. That's my love." shouted Jonathan within the crowd pointing at Nick first and then at Karolina. Some people in the crowd started laughing, but the others looked at Jonathan surprised.

"Yes, you heard me. He is nothing but a love-thief. He stole my love, my Karolina from me."

He looked down as if to cry.

"What are you doing here? You are not invited Jonathan."

Shouted Californika.

Jonathan staggered ahead as the crowd opened the way for him.

"Oh no! You are drunk again! You heard Cali, you were not invited nor are you welcome Jonathan."

He stopped and looked at Karolina.

"You can't say that. I.I. I. used to love you. I mean I love you."

He stopped and wore a frowned face.

"I just can't understand why I don't feel all that love I had for you."

He raised his face and looked at Nick.

"Don't look at me mate. I can't help on that. You can't walk away from love and expect to walk back in and find everything the way things were. She is mine now. My love now. Okay?"

Jonathan kept silent. He threw a quick glance at Nick before walking toward Karolina. Nick looked at Karolina with talking eyes. She raised her arm at the bodyguards who were now walking toward Jonathan. Tyler kept walking toward Jonathan.

"It's okay." shouted Karolina at one of the bodyguards.

Tyler a heavily built man stopped briefly and pointed at his waist belt before signaling to Dylan. Karolina squinted her eyes before looking at Jonathan.

"Let me talk to him." she shouted.

"Sorry I can't take chances, madam. I got to take him down."

"No! He will never hurt even a fly."

Tom whispered something into Cali's ear.

"He has a gun!" shouted Cali hiding behind Tom.

Jonathan got startled by the noise and shouting. It seemed he had been in a trance of some sort as he appeared disoriented.

"What?"

He shouted.

"Lie down on the ground now!" shouted Tyler.

Jonathan threw a quick glance at Nick. He pulled his gun from the trouser belt before aiming it at him.

"He is nothing but a love-thief."

He looked at Karolina.

"He stole my love. I don't know how."

"I know. Jonathan put the gun down. I will tell you"

She paused.

"You walked away from me even before I met him. He is a very good man. It happens! Sometimes you just stop loving someone. Nick has nothing to do with your heartbreak. Our love died. Okay."

Jonathan looked down and then at Nick.

"I am telling you. He stole my heart. He stole my love for you."

"Listen to yourself. How on earth can I steal your love you, pathetic loser? You forgot already? You walked away from her even before I met her. She is mine now. Get used to it."

"Shut up! You think I don't know? She is mine. That's my love."

"Used to be your love. Okay! But like I said, she is mine now. Correct me if I am wrong. You walked away from her it's not the other way around. Get it?"

"I said shut up! I love her!"

Nick smiled and walked toward Jonathan.

"Don't come near me or else I will shoot you."

"I am not afraid. Don't make me laugh. Do you love Karolina?"

"I love her."

Whispered Jonathan looking down.

"That's not the reply of a man in love. I ask you again. Do you love her? Do you love Karolina?"

There was a moment of hesitation. Everyone looked at him. Lost in thoughts. He touched his heart and looked at Karolina. He looked agonized.

"I can't feel the love I had for you my love."

"Oh no! She is my love now." shouted Nick.

Jonathan raised his gun up which he had just lowered and aimed at Nick.

"I swear I am going to shoot you if you don't shut up!" shouted Jonathan.

"Jonathan put the gun down! We can talk about this."

"He is a dangerous lunatic. What are the bodyguards looking at? Shoot him before he kills someone." shouted Cali.

"Don't say that Cali," advised Tom.

"This new boyfriend of yours does not love you."

"What? And you do?"

"Shut Up! You think I don't know what is going on here. You can fool everyone but not me. I know who sent you."

Karolina as soon as she heard that she covered her face.

"Listen Jonathan! You have suffered a heartbreak. You will be okay. Put the gun down. You need help."

"I don't need help. I want my love back. I love you. He can never love you the way I loved you."

"Yeah right in the past. This is now."

Jonathan ignored Nick and looked at Karolina.

"I have love for you. I loved you. Somehow, they stole my love. I can't feel my love for you."

"It happens love dies you know. Put the gun down we can go and talk okay."

"Listen to me!" shouted Nick.

"You are crossing the line now. Move on. She is mine. Wake up. This is the reality. You alone. Me with her."

"You, heart-thief. Maybe I shoot you. I know you stole my love."

Nick for the first time looked agitated and instantly pulled a gun sending the crowd screaming.

"Stay away from my woman before I put you out of your misery."

"I am not afraid."

"You think I am bluffing."

The bodyguards instantly pulled out their guns too and aimed at Jonathan. Karolina screamed. She ran toward Jonathan.

"Don't shoot. He is heartbroken. That's all. He will be okay. He is not dangerous. Don't shoot!"

"Stay away from my woman or I will shoot you." shouted Nick walking toward Jonathan at the same time gesturing to the body guards to stand down for a while.

"You walked away! Walk away now! You need help

not my love Karolina."

"She is mine. I still love her!"

"What? Do you still love her? Look in my face. Do you still love her?"

shouted Nick approaching even closer with a raised gun. Jonathan looked down and then at Karolina before touching his heart.

"Yes! So! Do you still love her? Answer me damn it!"

"I loved her?"

"I didn't hear you. I ask you again. Do... you... still... love... her?"

"No Nick don't shoot him!" shouted Karolina. Nick looked agitated and the anger patterns were evident in his voice. Jonathan knew that the man was now angry.

"You never understood her. You loved her I understand that. But I know also that that was in the past. You touch her, and I swear I will kill you. You had years with her. But like I said all in the past. Move on or I will kill you myself."

"I know the love you have is mine. My love which you stole from me?"

"Do you even know what you are talking about?"

"Don't be a smart ass with me. You can never have what we had."

Jonathan lowered his gun and looked at Karolina.

"Let's get back together again? What we had was real. Real love."

"That love also died last time I checked. You don't remember walking away? Did you suffer an amnesia or what?" shouted Cali.

"You stay out of this."

"Leave her alone. She moved on, you are a pathetic lunatic. You think you can walk out of someone and come back and expect everything to be okay? Are you crazy?"

"Karolina. I had love for you. Even though I can't feel anything right now, I know in my heart that I love you. I have always loved you and I will love you forever."

Californika laughed.

"Love her with what? Your heart is literally broken. You can never love again. You said it yourself."

"Who asked for your opinion?"

Jonathan touched Karolina's hand.

"Be careful or you will find yourself on the ground with a bullet hole in your forehead. Okay."

"My love I am going to show you that somehow the love he has for you is mine."

"What? Talk some sense Jonathan."

"Just know that I love you."

"Loved you. In the past. You lunatic," shouted Cali.

"I am tired of your stupid games. I will count to ten. Leave my girlfriend alone. Okay. She is with child."

Weeks later.

Jonathan entered the house he used to share with Karolina. He paced left and right before drawing a gun to his head.

"Why was he so sure that I don't love her?"

He whispered to himself.

"Maybe I am losing it. If they met after I walked away surely, he has nothing to do with this. Maybe I just shoot myself."

He slumped on the couch and cried for a while. He walked to the liquor cabinet and took out the whiskey. He poured some in a glass and downed a half-glass before putting on a squinted bitter face.

Nick arrived home from work and found Karolina slumped on the couch relaxing watching the television. He sat next to her before hugging her and kissing her all over. Nick was a very handsome man and less affectionate than Jonathan but a real man. He was not needy unlike Jonathan. Karolina was a very busy woman and any extra attention would have put a lot of strain on the relationship. Nick understood that, and that made their relationship unbreakable. Apart from having his own business and investments the couple were expecting a baby. Nick saw this as something to strengthen their relationship. They talked for a while before Nick started dosing off. Having slept for most of the day Karolina wasn't feeling sleepy at all. She enjoyed watching the television before the couple went to sleep and tonight was no different. A shadow of a man crossed past the window and she knew exactly who that was. Jonathan. What was he after this time? Surely now there was a real danger her being pregnant. Nick was not the kind of man who will let anyone mess up with his pregnant girlfriend. She quickly reached for the phone handset but then again thought for a while. She knew she had to tell Jonathan in a language he understands to stay away before things went out of control. Her heart started beating up. She looked at Nick. He was sleeping peacefully. She saw that shadow again before she heard a faint knock at the window. That's startled her even more.

"What the fuck does he think he is doing?" she thought out loud. She looked around. She knew where Nick kept his pistol. She also knew how Jonathan loved her. She cursed and swiftly got up and stealthily walked to the window and flipped the curtain. She was right. It was Jonathan standing outside the window. The sight of him gave her a turning stomach so bad that she felt sick. She thought out loud; was he out of his mind? Nick was determined to kill him if he is to find out that he was outside. She opened the door and walked outside to meet Jonathan.

"Are fucking crazy? What are you doing here? He will kill you if he sees you here. Do you want me to call the police or what? I told you never to come back here. Jonathan. What is going on?" she whispered.

Jonathan was very happy to see Karolina come outside. That brought some memories of the time they had together. The peak of their love. Karolina felt a warm nice feeling running down her spine. For a while she got lost as well. She felt Jonathan's love for her the days they were together. That was such a romantic time. Instantly without thought Jonathan carried Karolina into the air and swung around carrying her.

"Put me down. What are you doing? Jonathan. Put me down." She struggled at first before she started laughing secretly hanging onto him. She remembered the best times they had. She enjoyed that here and there especially now. Something Nick would never do. He was a gentleman not some crazy-in-love lunatic like Jonathan. She looked at Jonathan's face. For the first time in a long time his face shone with much happiness. She also remembered how excited his face became every time he talked about having kids with her. She also remembered how she has done everything to stop having a family early. She wanted to enjoy a kid-free-life. Nick was just lucky. He came at the right time and took the opportunity.

"I have some good news."

"What good news Jonathan?"

He looked at her while still lifting her up. She could still see the glittering in his eyes. The excitement and joy expressed on his face. She felt like she had just told him that she was pregnant. Somehow the pair found kissing and snogging each other.

"No! We can't do this. Put me down now before Nick comes out and shoot you.

"We can be together again."

She looked shocked and surprised at the same time. She wore a disbelieving face and looked at him.

"What? Are you fucking crazy? Where will Nick be? There can never be us again. The baby is not yours."

"I know I will look after you and our baby."

She could see the excitement in Jonathan's eyes. She remembered the best times they had. This is the man she fell in love with. Jonathan was very passionate and very crazy-in-love. She knew and remembered so many times he had lifted her up high in the air. It was romantic and very wonderful. She got lost in the heat of things too. Soon after the couple found snogging each other.

"I will look after you and our baby. I found a way, so we can be together again."

"What are you talking about there can never be you

and me again? I am with Nick now. Okay?"

"You once loved me. We can be together again Karo my love."

"Jonathan. I am with Nick."

"Nick! Nick? You mean that heart-thief."

Karolina wriggled holding and pushing away Jonathan's shoulders.

"I said put me down."

"Okay. Okay. I will put you down gently, there you go."

"We can be together again Karo my love."

Jonathan smiled. He held Karolina passionately and tried to kiss her.

"Why are you acting like a crazy fool?"

Jonathan stood there for a while. He looked troubled and afraid for a minute or two. He walked very close to Karolina who was walking away back to the house. He leaped forward holding her before she turns around.

"Listen to me Karo my love. Stay away from Nick. I don't know yet what he wants from you but whatever it is it's not good. I am sure he stole my love for you. Until I figure out what is going on can you please stay away from him. Promise me Karo."

He held Karolina's shoulder and looked at her straight into her shining blue eyes. Instantly the noise of the door opening sends both into a frightened state. A strong trembling voice cut through the otherwise silent night.

"Stay away from my love before I blow your brains out."

Karolina leaped in front of Jonathan.

"Nick don't shoot him! He came to tell me that he is going away. Okay, Jonathan?"

She turned and looked at Jonathan.

Jonathan looked upset and annoyed. He just looked at Karolina with a face that seemed to ask, what?

"I am not going anywhere. He is."

He looked at Nick with piercing eyes.

"What? And where am I going?" asked Nick a bit surprised and angry at the same time.

"To hell where you belong. You son of a beast! We were happy before you came."

"Sorry the baby is mine. Start walking away right now."

"Or else what? You, heart-thief?"

He pulled a gun too and aimed at Nick before a scream frightened both tearing the silent night. The barking of a dog introduced a break between the men's conversation for a while. The two men stood face-to-face guns in the hands. Karolina hysterically tried to stop the two men shooting each other.

"We were happy before you came. I had love for Karo. Life was great. We were always happy. We had everything we needed."

Nick laughed sarcastically and that annoyed Jonathan who instantly reacted by stretching his arm and holding the gun firm.

"What's funny? You think this is a joke? Maybe shoot you first."

"You just didn't understand her. Even now you don't know her that well."

"What are you talking about?"

"She never wanted all that. She wanted a man who really loves her. A man who can start a family with her. Not some crazy fool who don't even love her."

Jonathan's face creased with rage. He shook with anger as he pointed the gun at Nick. Karolina's scream pierced the night. Across the road a light in one of the bedrooms came on diverting the focus and attention of the two men.

"Don't talk nonsense. I loved her! You son of a beast!"

"Exactly! Loved her! Not now!"

"Shut up! I love her."

"What! Do you really love her? Did I hear you correctly? Did you just say you love her?"

"That's right! I love her?"

"You are getting me worried and upset now because you are lying. We both know you have no love for her. Do you walk away from people you love?"

"Shut up!"

Jonathan lowered the gun down and looked at Karolina.

"I just don't know what happened but whatever it is I bet you had everything to do with it."

"Please! She just chose a better man."

"Better man? You? Ha! You mean bloody heart-thief."

"If it wasn't for Karo, I could have shot you. She is pregnant and stay away okay. Go now and stay away from my girlfriend."

Karolina walked toward Jonathan and held his arm pushing him away.

"Go. I am with Nick now. If you love me, you will respect my wishes."

"No! Stay away from him. I don't know what he is after but whatever it is it is not good."

"We are expecting a baby now okay so go?"

Jonathan stopped and looked at Karolina.

"He is not good for you. I just know it?"

Nick started walking toward them.

"And you are good for her? How can you be? You

left her alone crying herself to sleep? Tell me right now how you are better? Right now, you just said it yourself that you have no love for her. So how can you say that?"

"You stole it."

Nick leaped forward and punched Jonathan so hard that he stumbled and fell backward. He got up and turned around and aimed the gun at Nick. Nick with an angry face looked at Jonathan with piercing eyes, unmoved nor afraid. Karolina screamed in desperation as soon as she heard a click made by the cocking up of the gun.

CHAPTER TWO

A loud scream woke up the neighbors. Instantly a dog barked hysterically miles away. Karolina sat on the bed frightened. Nick lifted his head and looked at his chest with an agonized face. He screamed in pain. He touched his heart and lifted his head again before slumping on the bed.

"Ah my chest. Oh my God!"

Karolina sobbing looked at Nick for a split second before getting up and getting the phone.

"Come on pick up!" she whispered.

The phone rung for a while before a voice answered on the other end.

"Come quickly,"

The person on the other end didn't say anything. As

soon as he heard the stress patterns in Karolina's voice, the doctor Dr. Hughes knew it straight away that it was an emergency call.

"The doctor is on the way. Hang in there, darling. Everything will be okay." said Karolina beside Nick who was wriggling in pain on the bed. The look on his face said it all. He was in agony. He clutched his chest and looked at Karolina. Sweat droplets trickled down his face and neck before disappearing on the bed-sheets. His eyes instantly closed as he squinted in pain. Karolina simply watched not knowing what to do. Instantly Nick snapped open his eyes. He looked at Karolina before looking on his chest. The sound of a car engine outside caught Karolina's attention. Instantly she got up and ran toward the door. Soon afterward Karolina and the doctor entered the bedroom. Nick had stopped moving. Sweat beads formed on his forehead before rolling down his face. He had an abnormal heart beat. The doctor looked at him and then at Karolina before kneeling next to him. He started checking his vitals. Karolina looked at him with asking eyes. He looked at her and nodded his head. The pair looked at Nick. He lay there without moving but his eyes were moving rapidly under the closed eyelids. His eyes were moving very quickly. His side temple veins had a high pressure that they could easily see the veins' movements as the blood thumbs past. The doctor looked at his chest. He was hyperventilating. His heart beat was beating very fast making his whole body, stomach and ribs to react to the vibrations.

"Is he going to be alright?"

The doctor continued checking Nick first.

"I guess so I have to stabilize him first," replied the doctor.

Nick's eyes instantly stopped moving underneath the closed eyelids. The doctor looked at Karolina first before looking at Nick. He lowered his head to Nick's chest level. He lifted his head and checked inside his bag. He touched Nick's chest and instantly Nick breathed faintly before his eyes started moving again underneath the closed eyelids.

Later Nick lay peacefully on the bed. Karolina sat next to him on the bed. She looked at him.

"What's happening darling?"

She sobbed rubbing her stomach.

She looked at Nick and instantly tears rushed out from her eyes. Tear drops soaked the bed-sheets near him.

"I love you very much. I just don't know what I will do if something bad happened to you."

She sobbed and took out her handkerchief and blew her nose. She lay on top of Nick's half-naked body. She lifted her head and looked at him.

His eyes were still moving very fast underneath the

closed eyelids. He seemed to have stabilized as he was breathing normal. She planted kisses on his forehead, the cheeks and lips. She lay her head on his raised hairy chest and she closed her eyes. She could hear his heart beat rate. She remembered the first days they met. It was magical. The more she thought about it the more the tears trickled down her cheeks onto his rigged chest.

In her subconscious mind she felt Nick's chest movements and heartbeat instantly stop. She opened her eyes and lifted her head from Nick's chest and looked at him. The eyes were moving very fast under the closed eyelids. He had somehow stopped breathing, or she thought. Instantly Nick's eyelids snapped open. He looked at Karolina with wide-opened eyes, haunted and disoriented. He instantly lifted his head and with a creased agonized face he looked at his chest and touched it. He breathed heavily and loudly before slumping on the bed. He breathed out air and instantly looked calm as his eyes met Karolina's. He smiled as he saw her gorgeous face. He lay calmly looking at her.

Karolina looked at him before quickly hugging him lying on top of him kissing him everywhere.

"I am glad you are okay darling."

She planted kisses on his lips when he tried to talk she placed her index finger on his lips. She kissed him on his cheeks, neck and rigged chest passionately. She pulled her dress up and jumped on top of him sitting on his crotch.

"What happened!"

He asked disoriented for a while. He touched his chest and looked at the inside of his hand.

"It's going to be alright. The doctor said that you were probably having a nightmare. Everything is going to be alright."

She rubbed herself on his well-defined body kissing him everywhere passionately. She pulled her dress up to her head level and removed it.

"I love you."

She looked at him.

He still looked worried and disoriented.

"The doctor said that everything is going to be okay. Just a nightmare or something but nothing to worry about."

Nick scanned the whole bedroom and then looked at Karolina.

"Just a nightmare. I thought..."

"Shh don't talk darling."

Karolina unfastened her bra and took it off before rubbing her body onto Nick's.

Nick breathed heavily.

"Karo."

Karolina paused and got up and looked at him. That somehow sounded very strange. She hadn't heard Nick call her by her first name for a very long time. It was always darling, sweetheart, honey, my-better-half, etc. She looked at him. She noticed something for the first time. His face was emotionless. He looked dull, unloving and frightened. After a quick thought she looked at him and kissed him.

"You are going to be alright darling. Okay. Nothing to worry about."

"I know Karo. Just a nightmare."

"I love you Nick. Very much. Even more than I did before. At one point I thought you suffered a heart attack or something. I was very scared. Never scared that way before. I thought I was going to lose you."

"I know," replied Nick trying to get up while touching his heart area.

"No. The doctor said you need to lie in bed for more time to gather back your strength."

"I need to get up I am feeling aches for lying down for too long."

Nick struggled to get up but eventually managed to sit down. He looked at Karolina for a while before planting a kiss on her forehead. He breathed heavily and staggered out of the bedroom. Karolina slumped on the bed half-naked. She lay there peacefully. She looked at the bedroom dressing table and all that she could hear was the ticking of the dressing table clock. She looked at the time and somehow found the clock very beautiful.

"Darling don't forget today we are visiting my parents. I think it's a great opportunity to get away from all this. Time to relax and wind down for a few days."

"Oh, it's this week, yes?"

"Yes darling."

"Karolina, I don't think I want to travel..."

"But we planned this a long time ago darling."

"I know Karo. I just think I am not ready to travel far away." He paused and touched his chest and looked at Karolina.

"Ooh I see. But darling there is nothing to be afraid of. It was just a horrible nightmare."

Nick walked in the bedroom before sitting on the bed.

"What if that happens again, away from home?"

"Don't let that stop you living your life."

"I know babe, but I am comfortable here at home. We can postpone and go later when I am feeling better."

"No, we have to go as planned darling."

"Maybe go on your own. It should be alright."

Karolina stopped and realized that maybe she was being selfish. She breathed heavily and sat on the corner of the bed.

"I thought ..."

"I am just not feeling myself. Maybe go on your own. We can always go together in the future."

"No darling we have to go together. We need to deliver the great news together too."

Karolina touched her stomach and smiled before landing a smacker on Nick's cheek.

A sport utility vehicle [SUV] left a mansion and turned into the main road before speeding away. Nick looked at his wife-to-be on the passenger seat. It was a very beautiful sunny day. It was hot. They both wore sunglasses. Karolina was wearing a thin lovely pink maternity dress. She looked fabulous even in the maternity dress. A small bulging stomach was protruding. Every time Nick looked at the pregnant stomach he smiled. Every time they looked at each other it was all smiles. Very romantic. Karolina's face suddenly sunken. Nick looked at her and instantly looked ahead as he was driving. He put his hand on her lap and gently stroked her and smiled. He looked at the dashboard and played the Carolinadeivid song Seductive Beauty.

"You like this song very much. Very sweet and romantic. I remember the first days."

"That's the reason I bought this album. Reminds me of the best days we had."

There was silence but only the background song Seductive Beauty.

"Just like in the song the first time I saw you I knew I had to make you mine. Somehow my wish fulfilled. Very romantic."

Nick smiled.

Karolina smiled too.

"I know. That first night, it was very nice."

"I remember whisking you away from all the others. Great dancer I must admit."

The couple listened to the song for a while.

"If it wasn't for the dancing, we might not have clicked."

"I agree but I think it was just meant to be anyway."

"I am glad you said that."

"Don't you still feel the same?"

"I love you I am just saying..."

She looked at Nick and sighed.

Nick sensed the tension and worries.

"You can tell me. What is it?"

"I was afraid you no longer feel the same way."

"Don't be silly how on earth can you even think like

that? I love you and will always do. Are you confusing me with your crazy ex, Jonathan?"

Karolina removed the sunglasses and looked at Nick.

"You know why I loved you at first sight?"

"Go on."

"You were different. You were romantic and very passionate and considerate."

"Hang on, stop there. You are using past tense."

"You changed Nick. You have never called me by my first name before. What happened? What happened to; Darling? Sweetheart? Honey? Babes?"

Nick as a reflex stepped on the gas and the SUV roared moving faster, all they could hear was the sound of the engine eating away the sound of the background song. He panted.

"I haven't changed darling. That day changed everything. I thought I almost died. I was just worried that has nothing to do with my love for you. You know I love you and will always do."

Nick reached for Karolina's hand and touched her passionately.

"I am glad to hear that. I was worried."

It was not long before the SUV turned into a narrow road that took them through the surrounding trees until they reached a beautiful house on its own surrounded by beautiful botanic gardens.

"It's beautiful. Great atmosphere. A breath of fresh air and exciting scenery."

"Great place to wind down. You will love it. Come."

A limousine parked outside one of the buildings in the city center. The usher walked out swiftly from the building to the limousine and instantly opened the door. A man dressed-to-kill in an expensive suite got out of the limousine. The usher stopped and admired him for a while. The man stopped and straightened his suite jacket and tie and with his saliva moistened his smartly styled hair. He smelled, looked and walked a million dollars. He was the best there can be. Rich and flamboyant. He was no ordinary man. The usher got lost for a while admiring this man. He looked at his suit and then the shoes and thought. Probably the shoes alone were worth more than the usher was wearing and if not including himself. He thought briefly.

"Those must be expensive shoes," he whispered.

"Sorry this way," he shouted.

The man walked with style toward one of the buildings. A swift knock and the huge door opened.

"I was expecting you glad you finally came."

"It must be very important requesting my services at such a short notice,"

"Please come in."

Brayden a very handsome and masculine man in his

early thirties with short and sleek hair walked in and sat comfortably on the sofa in the office. He instantly lifted one of his legs onto the other and straightened his tie. He looked a million-dollars even Tyler knew Brayden was not cheap. Whatever it was it must be big to require Brayden services.

"Have you been addressed regarding this project?"

"You can say that," replied Brayden confidently.

"Well then without wasting your time let's get down to business. Shall we?"

Tyler a man in his late forties struggled to open the safe and not because it was difficult. No. Brayden had put pressure on him for he wanted to feel important and special as well. He took his time trying to make his job feel important to Brayden. He finally opened the safe and took out a shoe box and placed it on the table. Inside was a rolled letter like item. A quick pull of the flaps of the ribbon and all were smiles. Tyler removed the item from the cloth slowly and carefully and gave it to Brayden. The item rolled open in Brayden's hand.

"What is this?" asked Brayden.

"The list Sir."

Brayden wore a troubled face.

"Why do I need a list for. They told me I am here to pick a file for one person."

Tyler did not reply but instead shrugged off his

shoulders. Brayden looked at the list before his face creased with confusion. He walked out of the office building. He jumped back in the limousine before the limousine disappeared.

CHAPTER THREE

"I can't believe you even said that?"

There was silence in the room.

Oliver's face blushed and creased with anger and rage. He appeared to be choking with rage as his eyes turned red.

"How can you say that? Did you see how they slaughtered innocent women and children."

There was a brief silence.

"I am just saying don't be too quick to judge."

"Don't make me angry. Don't just say things for the sake of it. I know what I am talking about. They ripped open pregnant women and children. You heard the General, they have fallen below standards."

"The General has no tangible evidence to support his remarks. I am just saying it will be hard to prove."

"Hard to prove or not! This is below standards. I have watched them for the past seventeen years. It can never be lower than this. What are you waiting for? They were swift to attack for lesser crimes than this. I say we should reciprocate. Swift and ruthless and match their actions."

"Oliver! Listen! We need tangible evidence. We need to convince everyone or else tomorrow it will be our turn."

Oliver punched the table with the side of his hand very hard that papers flew in the air before landing on the office carpet.

"Don't talk nonsense. They are just going to destroy all the evidence just like before. I say to hell with the evidence. We have seen a lot for the past seventeen years. Just look! All the data erased, just a few days ago. I say we contact the others and invade."

Bryson looked scared for a while. He had never seen Oliver that upset before. Surely something big was on the cards. It seemed the table had turned. The world before today had turned a blind-eye, but it seemed time was catching up with them. This was the worst for the past seventeen years. They had become so complacent and arrogant that things had fallen way below what was expected. Oliver had seen the attack. It was like yesterday. It was so vivid in his mind that at times he had panic attacks just thinking about this. Even though he was young when it happened. It was a day he will never forget. Even now, more often he would look inside the palm of his hands and can still see the blood. It was horrific, worse for a kid like him to see people being slaughtered that way. Even now it hasn't sunk in. How all his small-town people ended up the sheep for the slaughter. He had no idea who the General was. He had no clue how his small-town people ended up dead because of the General's crimes. He remembered all the people talk badly about this General. Honestly even they, they disliked this General. He was even mean to them. Stealing the little they had before killing the men in their town. It was like a double edged-sword piercing them when they got attacked because of this General. A person they despised. It was horrific. For Oliver it was the worst day in his life. He lost all his family. He remembered seeing people begging for mercy only for bullets to be lodged in their temples.

"I say we invade. An eye for an eye. Remember? We should revenge. This is the only way to heal the pain and anguish suffered those days."

"Oliver. I am with you. I know you are hurting but I think we need a diplomatic solution."

A big bang was instantly heard and papers on the table flew in the air in slow motion. Bryson looked at them before they landed on the ground. Oliver's face bloated with rage. His once blue eyes had instantly turned to blood-red color.

"Diplomatic solution! Why they didn't do the same! They were swift to invade and slaughter our people. I say we do the same. A cheek for a cheek. You must get out!"

Bryson breathed heavily.

"We don't want others to be in this situation. When will this stop? We invade with swiftness and tomorrow someone will raise your issues too. People will keep dying."

"I don't care. What about the blood that was spilled? Who will quench the wailing souls? The spirits haven't rested. There is restlessness. Too much evil still going on. We need a conclusion to all this and that can only be achieved if we match evil with evil."

"I understand. I feel your pain too."

"No! You don't!!"

Bryson kept quiet for a while whilst Oliver raged.

"Did you see innocent women and kids die?"

Bryson did not answer. He could only look down.

"I saw women beg for their lives. I saw helpless kids being shot at point-blank. So, don't tell me you feel my pain. Everyone knows they have fallen below standard.

"I am doing my best."

"Your best? You think this is a joke. You should have

listened to me. Invade! A test of their own medicine. We could be in a better position now. All your fault. Look seventeen years now and they have only become more devious and cleverer and manipulating. Just imagine the pain and suffering for the past seventeen years. Still no change. You should have listened. If you hadn't stepped in today, things could be for the better. You cost us lives and precious time. There are some things not to negotiate and this is one of them. There is no room for negotiations. So, don't waste more of our time and lives. You leave now. Escape as planned."

"But..."

"Listen this is not negotiable. They will never change."

"Sir. With all due respect the main idea behind me negotiating was for us to gather enough evidence so we bring them to the international court."

"Seventeen years! What do you have?"

Bryson stood up and walked toward the window.

"You are right there. Nothing, but I think we can still bring them to the court."

"You know that can be another ten years? Who has that time? You saw it yourself they erased the documents submitted just a few days ago."

Bryson breathed heavily before sitting down.

"You know I have a point. Time for negotiations is

over. Send the word. Leave now. Once you are out, we will invade swiftly and ruthlessly. Like I have been saying evil can only breed evil."

"But I sent all the documents to the court can we at least wait for the court's decision."

"You haven't heard!"

"Heard what?" asked Bryson.

"Judge Kaden died of blood-sugar this morning?"

Bryson sunk in his chair and looked at Oliver.

"Excuse me I have to make a phone call." said Bryson getting up.

Miles away a couple were watching the news.

Seth a man in his forties was in the lounge area with his girlfriend Jacqueline.

"Just in. Armed men have entered the bank in broad daylight and ordered everyone down before leaving with hundred thousands of dollars if not millions. Surprising no one called the authorities until after the robbers had long gone. The manager of the bank is under criticism today and many hope and wish that he should lose his job over the incident. The men are believed to have ordered everyone to cooperate at gunpoint. Even if this is the case it took minutes for those involved to have called the authorities. No one was shot. Often most expected someone to have called the authorities soon after. This is one of the strange occurrences that have hit the cities across the country. Susan reporting for Touchladybirdlucky Studios."

Jacqueline sat up straight and looked at Seth.

"Have I heard correctly? I find that very strange. How can the bank staff get robbed and no one alert the authorities soon after the robbers had left?"

"Odd but there could be a lot of reasons to explain that?"

"Seth! What reasons?"

"I don't know. Maybe they threatened them?"

"But they said that they alerted the authorities long after the robbers had gone."

"I don't know babe."

A knock at the door of the bank manager's office startled Mr. Trenton the bank manager.

The door suddenly opened, and Mr. Trenton came face-to-face with Detective Braden. A young detective late twenties with well shaven face with dark long hair.

"Don't worry it's just me."

Mr. Trenton's face changed from a haunted face to a welcoming face.

"Come in Detective. What a relief. I have been through a lot. Just don't think I can go through that again and survive. They nearly blasted me at point-blank."

The detective walked in and looked around. He looked at the bank manager and retrieved a small pager like device. He retracted a pen attached on the side and pointed at the screen.

"Don't get me wrong. I understand what you have been through but...."

He paused and sat down.

"Yes, go on Detective."

"All the people I asked said there was no struggle at all. Most didn't panic as they might have had in other robbery situations. To put it in one of the witnesses' words it was like a collection if you know what I mean rather than a bank robbery. What do you say to that?"

Mr. Trenton's face creased as his eyes squinted.

"What are you implying Detective?"

"I am just saying there was no struggle at all. Lets' see..."

"Do you struggle with people holding guns Detective? They were armed. They said cooperate and live, struggle and die."

The detective coughed slightly clearing his throat.

"Even in the given circumstances it took you more than twenty minutes to call for help."

"We did what we can do in the given circumstances. Maybe that's why also that no one was shot or killed for that matter. We were just afraid."

"It seemed also that no emergence buttons were activated when the robbers were still in the vicinity why is that? Isn't it your job to alert the authorities as soon as possible?"

"It happened so fast my main concern was with the safety of the people."

"But still you have a duty to alert the authorities so that we try to trace these robbers as soon as possible."

"Not trying to be funny Detective I did what I can in the given circumstance."

"Have they threatened your family, threatened to come back for you, threatened you personally?"

Mr. Trenton looked surprised for a while.

"No Detective. They just walked in with guns and demanded that we cooperate."

"But still you should have followed protocol. Increase the chances of these robbers getting caught by alerting us quickly."

"That I will leave to you Detective. They did not destroy any CCTV cameras, and they were recording the time they robbed us. That's why I did not panic I know it was only a matter of time before you get them."

The detective looked surprised and confused.

"Are you sure the cameras were working? What kind of robbers are they? Stealing all that money? Leaving clues behind?"

"There you go that can explain also my reactions. I thought they were bluffing."

The detective retrieved his cellphone and dialed a number.

"Okay, Mr. Trenton. I think I must watch the CCTV footage first. I will be in touch."

The detective walked to the door and was about to go outside the bank managers' office.

"One last thing. Are you sure they did not threaten you personally? Not related? Do you know any of them?"

"What are you implying Detective? Like I said they did not threaten me directly."

Detective Kristy a tall slim attractive and fit woman with long but nicely tied blonde hair entered the office. She sat down before her cellphone started ringing.

"Yes Braden. What's up. What did you get?"

"You won't believe it. Either they are amateurs or very cocky. They left the CCTV untouched."

"Yeah. I still recall all witnesses saying they were wearing masks! So, no big deal. Give me something I can use Braden."

"This is something. Surely, we must watch the footage. We might get clues. A tattoo or something. I don't know. Get the evidence processed quickly. I have a gut feeling that there must be something we can use."

"Come on Braden. What did the others get? Didn't they have the CCTV footage? I need something I can use. An electronic-Fit or a witness statement or something."

"I am on my way there."

Soon after the line went dead.

Detective Kristy was startled by her pager.

"Sugar!! Son of a beast," she cursed.

She looked at the pager and soon left the office. She walked in the long corridor ignoring Detective Paxton's taunting. A brief knock at the door and the door was swayed wide open. Inside were two other detectives.

A man smartly dressed opened the parked car door and got out as soon as another car approached from the other side. He pulled down the suite jacket and straightened his bow tie. He moisturized the tips of his fingers and slightly stroked his hair. He had a sleek clean shave. He felt a million-dollars as evidenced by the way he walked. The look on his face said it all. This was no other day. It was a very important day in his life. At sixteen he had dropped out of college.

This was his first job interview. He was excited, very excited at the prospects of becoming a working-class citizen. He worried if he had made the right decision; dropping out of college. The car stopped and Cynthia, a very attractive lady got out of the car dressed-to-kill in a short dress. The couple were in each other's hands in no time.

"Thanks for coming. This means a lot to me. I am ready."

Cynthia smiled and landed a kiss on his lips before they walked toward the office blocks. Bradley opened his eyes and looked around. He was in a luxurious hotel room. He could hear the shower water. Ever since getting his new job life had never been the same again. His job could mean him in a different city every weekend the main thing he loved the most. He knew this was very healthy for their relationship with Cynthia. Dynamic and different. The company paid for everything. He knew he had made the right decision dropping out of college. The past three years had been the best he had had. Suddenly the shower water stopped running, and he heard Cynthia's shouting something from the bathroom.

"What did you say darling?" asked Bradley.

Cynthia entered the hotel bedroom with a towel round her body.

"I said I want to go shopping."

"You know I have to do my job first."

"I know. I can go on my own. I need to stretch my legs anywhere."

"That's alright darling."

Cynthia left the hotel room and headed to the city center for shopping leaving Bradley doing his work.

Bradley got out his laptop and started typing. He connected an external hard drive and kept typing. He paused and looked around thinking. He noticed Cynthia's bra under the bed. He smiled and pondered his life with Cynthia. He remembered the day of the job interview. She had stood by him. Life had been a blessing since then. She had trusted him from the very first day they met. She was completely different from Sienna. Sienna was the most beautiful girl he had laid eyes on. She was very beautiful and a perfectionist. She was like an angel with everything small, a small nose that made her accent sound sweet and sexy with small perfect lips as compared to Cynthia's. She wanted everything to be perfect. All she talked about was getting married first before even contemplating sleeping together. To Bradley she was the ultimate dream girl for him but to be honesty getting married was a very remote idea for him. He had dropped college at sixteen with no prospect of finding a job or any concrete plans of how he was going to support himself let alone miss-angel-Sienna. Even the talk of marriage at that age made him resent the idea. Later he found his love for Sienna changing with every date they had. He had a lot to deal with and Sienna kept pushing and comparing their relationship to others. The day he met Cynthia was after one of their burst-ups. He had walked away. He knew, or should I say he hadn't anticipated to be as successful as he ended up being. Sienna was a high maintenance lady with a huge taste of the best life had to offer. Too much pressure. Complains after complaints had driven him mad. He knew he had to let her go and let her have a man who she deserved. Someone rich enough. Someone who understood her. He knew he had to let her go. It wasn't easy though. He truly loved her. In fact, he loved her very much to let her go. He knew it that he was never going to make her happy. They loved each other no doubt. It's just the pressure that was too much for him. The expectations were very high. He remembered crying himself to sleep the day he walked away from her. But somehow, he found solace in her complaints that he never really felt how much he loved her until years later. I guess her complaints had suppressed his feelings for her that it was easy to walk away but he truly loved her. He remembered the look in her eyes that one afternoon. She was the woman of his dreams. The love of his life yet he managed to walk away from her leaving her standing there in tears. It was such a traumatic day for both. They had just quarreled. He had no job. He had just dropped out of college. She had thrown the million-dollar question. How was he going to provide for them let's say if he got her pregnant? He knew she had a point. It was a question he had no answers to. It was a question he had been asking himself. He looked at her. He saw the passion in her eyes. He could read that face like a book. He knew he had to leave her. He had nothing to offer. In life sometimes, there are situations when just love is not enough. She was like an angel. She deserved the best life had to offer. She had cried numerous times in his arms. All the tears and complaints were starting to show. He knew he would dislike himself if that angelic face was to change for the worse because of him. He knew to love her was to let her go. To love her was to exchange happiness for her for his selfish dreams. Another day another cry was to leave scares on that gorgeous face of hers something he never wanted to associate himself with. Bradley although he struggled during his early years he understood and valued beauty, probably the main reason Sienna loved him in the first place. He knew God created some on days when he had a lot of energy and very enthusiastic that he ended up showing off and that was one of the days he created Sienna. Everything about her was in perfect detail. He remembered the first time he laid eyes on her. He could see God himself. The way she was brought up had a lot to do with her attitude as well and probably the main reason behind her complaints. To Bradley the things she considered as basic, a huge house, a car, a good education and all the best life has to offer were dear things you must sweat for. Now that he had everything even though that seemed distant those days. He sometimes wondered what if he had stayed with her through thin and thick? He knew she was right but at the same time he never really regretted it. He had put her happiness first something he would not trade for even today. It was the ringing of the phone that startled him and woken him up from this dream.

"Hello! Who is this?"

The person on the other side of the phone spoke in what seemed to be a foreign language. Soon after a beep sound alerted him that it was an international call and that the conversation will be translated after and that to keep holding the line. The message went on for some time before the English translation.

"Hello Mr. Bradley. This is a security message to alert you that your account has been accessed and funds have been transferred from your account."

"Hello, are you sure the message is for me?"

Bradley placed the receiver down briefly.

"Automated message."

He quickly took out his cellphone and dialed the number showing on the hotel's phone receiver.

The number was an international number.

"Hello. I just received a call from this number. What is this place?"

The person replied in a foreign Baltic language.

"Hello."

The person on the other end asked for Bradley to hold the line and there was silence for a while. Later another person this time a woman spoke on the line in English.

"This is the headquarters of the bank. Can I have your account and reference number?"

Bradley looked surprised and confused.

"Has the headquarters moved? Last time I checked the headquarters was in the States."

"If you give me the account number, I will be able to help you."

Bradley looked surprised and quickly retrieved a card from his wallet and gave the account number and reference number. The woman typed and punched figures quickly.

"Yes Mr. Bradley. We send a security alert every time you transfer money from your account especially if you transfer the maximum limit."

Bradley laughed and pulled his laptop close to himself.

"Maximum? Did she buy a plane or what?"

The woman interrupted instantly.

"I don't know you tell me it's your account."

"Sorry I was just thinking out loud. Could this be a mistake or a false alarm? I don't think she will need that kind of money. Still, I don't see how that's possible even though we share the account, the alerts go to her cellphone."

The woman paused a while and punched the keyboard.

"The message is correct. $100 000 has been transferred out today."

Bradley stopped looking at the laptop screen and shouted.

"$100 000?"

CHAPTER FOUR

A motorcade of black SUVs and a black limousine lined the street before entering a compound in the city center. The doors opened, and a woman dressed in a suite entered the building. A man holding folders followed her walking very fast to keep up with her pace.

"What is it? What are we looking at?"

"I can't say for sure, but we are looking at a legal case."

"I don't understand. Jaylen assured me the designs I mean everything was ours how come on earth are we even having this conversation."

"I think Jaylen is better suited to answer you,

madam."

"He better have a good explanation for all this."

The woman walked fast into the office without knocking. The look on her face said it all. Something big had come up and by the sound of her voice patterns it was not good at all. Jaylen rose from his seat and pointed at the comfy sofa in his office. The woman looked unamused by his presence. She did not sit but instead walked to the window and flipped open the curtain rail. She looked outside.

"Jaylen do you know how important is trust and reputation in political circles? Surely if you try to destroy my career this way I will ruin your life, the life of your kids and all your grandchildren. Do you know that?"

Jaylen nodded.

"What? You can't even talk?"

"I understand, madam, I still..."

He did not finish talking before the woman interrupted.

"How did this happen? If the designs were ours how come they already have a finished prototype?"

"I swear. The idea was mine. The designs mine too."

"So how on earth can they have an already finished design when we haven't even finished building ours?"

Jaylen looked haunted.

"All I can say is that I don't know but I will find out how this happened."

"Find out when? You mean when you have destroyed my career?"

"No, madam. I don't know how they got my designs, but I will find out."

"Legality?"

"Still issues. I haven't fully finished the designs to have patented them. So tricky as well."

"Jaylen. Let me tell you something. In politics there are no buts. Misrepresentation is the biggest killer of many politicians. I think I made this clear from day one."

"I know, madam."

"So, what are you saying?"

"Hacked."

"I thought you said our system is solid?"

"Now to be honest I don't know. I can't think of any idea how they did this."

Later Jaylen paced left, right and left in his office before a knock on the door startled him.

"Come in!"

The door opened instantly.

"What seems to be the problem my friend?"

asked Shawn.

"Bastards. They are my designs. My ideas. Everything all mine."

Jaylen angrily walked to the window and looked outside before turning around to face Shawn.

"All the designs mine. I can't just figure out how they did this?"

"Maybe this time you are wrong my friend. This time there was a faster thinking brain than yours. Mind you they have a finished prototype already when you are still in the drawing and designing room. No matter how this is not what you want to hear, you lost my friend."

"Even if it was not my design what are the chances that they will develop theirs to exact measurements as mine?"

"So, can we still go ahead as planned?

"Shawn my friend I don't think it's a good idea anymore. The senator has withdrawn the funds. She does not want to associate herself with any controversy. She has a lot to lose than me."

"So that's it,"

"I guess so. No funds no project."

Bradley remembered the screen that quickly popped-up on his laptop. There was no mistake what it was. He thanked himself that he had acted quickly and captured the screen seconds before it disappeared. Ever since, that had been nagging him for a while now. That morning he had jumped into his car and drove away without a word leaving Cynthia with a lot of questions. He looked at the dashboard for a split second before opening the laptop. He looked at the screen and looked ahead. The car turned into a private road and slowly urged forward before coming to a halt. Bradley got out and walked toward the huge building. Hesitantly and breathing heavily he stopped at the huge gates. He entered some codes into the gate screen.

"Access denied,"

Instantly a camera turned and pointed at him.

A voice from the gate's public address [PA] system startled him.

"You have no authorization to access these premises."

Bradley murmured something.

He looked down for a while and thought.

Quickly he took out his wallet and retrieved a card. He flashed the card.

"Classified but I am working here today."

The camera zoomed on him before a crackling sound startled him further.

"Enter your ID number."

Shaking Bradley entered the code.

"Wait there someone will come for you."

Bradley's heart paced fast with every second.

He looked around and then at the camera still pointing at him. The gate opened slowly, and a smartly dressed up man came out. He didn't say anything much apart from asking Bradley to follow him.

Bradley's heart beat very fast as he walked inside. Every step he made the camera turned on him. He looked at the red flashing light on every camera. No doubt this was a secured area. Bradley looked at the man ahead of him. He walked like a soldier straight, upright and fast with every step planned perfectly. As soon as he arrived at the door to a huge room, he stopped swiftly and turned instantly and looked at Bradley before pushing the door open.

"Wait in here I will be right back. Sir.!"

Bradley did not reply but instead peeped inside and entered quickly. As soon the man had disappeared Bradley quickly opened his handbag and retrieved his laptop. He switched it on quickly and looked at the saved document. He looked around and saw a camera pointing where he was seated. There was an instant jump in his heart beat. He quickly got up and walked out of the room and into the corridor. He looked everywhere as fast as he can before one corridor lead him to the other. He glanced at the laptop screen before looking around. He turned around and pushed open the closed door. He stopped and looked around before going through a passage into another room until he reached the stairs. He looked around and saw an elevator. He entered the elevator that took him to the floors below. A corridor led him to the room with the red door. He entered his access codes and waited nervously.

The "Access denied," message appeared on the LCD screen of the door.

He quickly opened his laptop and punched in some figures very fast.

"Video-sender."

He whispered as a moving circle appeared on followed by an instant message.

"Searching and linking to video network system."

He looked around as the moving circle on the screen appeared and disappeared.

"Come on."

He shouted.

After a while a beep sound startled him.

"Choose the correct option below."

Message appeared on the screen.

"Choose virtual connection."

He punched the enter button.

"Enter virtual access codes,"

Quickly Bradley entered his access codes.

A virtual screen quickly appeared.

Inside the screen was a huge oval room with computers everywhere. He searched for a computer that was used last and retrieved information of the user.

He entered the information on his laptop and recreated the last session. He waited for the computer to synchronize the coordinates and using the time-space continuum noted the time the last user left the room. He moved back in time and space and got the likely access codes used. He retrieved a small box from his pocket and tried all the codes displayed. The first one yielded the access denied message. He tried all the likely codes again and again and finally the door suddenly opened.

He closed the laptop and entered inside. The room was huge than it had appeared on the virtual screen. Inside there were computers and screens all over the place. At the center was a huge monitor and a desk. The screens and the computers were all switched on and a lot of information and CCTV images were being displayed. A loud humming sound caught his attention coming from a room next to this huge room. He walked toward the room and slid open the door. Inside were heavy industrial-like computers capturing a lot of data. He paused and thought for a while.

"Wait, a minute."

He stopped and thought.

He quickly opened his laptop and logged on.

He linked to the video-sender and connected to the network. After a while he could access all computers and phones network within a certain radius. He clicked on show the network screens within the radius.

A list of more than a 100 computer screens, cellphones and televisions within the radius instantly appeared. He realized that this is what he was paid to do as a profession only that here it was on an enormous scale. He breathed heavily and connected to the room's network. A list of a hundred thousand if not millions appeared on the huge screen in the room. He walked to the screen and sat on the computer desk in the middle. He breathed heavily and punched in some coordinates on the keyboard. A message instantly appeared.

The computers listed everyone's cellphone, computer and television activities.

"Bloody thieves."

Shouted Bradley.

The ringing of his cellphone startled him.

"What is it Cynthia? I can't talk right now."

"I think someone is following me. Where are you?"

"I think I found the answers."

"Answers to what?"

"Remember we talked about my job?"

"Yes."

"I know now why they were paying me loads of money."

There was silence.

"Are they doing something wrong? Is that why someone is after me?"

Cynthia felt a cold shiver down her spine.

"So?"

"Yes. I think they hacked into everyone's computer, cellphone and television system."

"I still can't see how that is worth a hundred thousand if not million dollars."

"I guess they hack into everyone's system without the person's knowledge and monitors their activities."

"Still not worth a billion dollars?"

"Here is how they make billion dollars. They steal people's designs, ideas and anything they are working on and sell the ideas first."

"Bradley still that can't explain everything."

"This is a sophisticated institutionalized project with huge resources and manpower behind it. They steal people's ideas and advance these making them their own. They have a huge resources base and connections."

Cynthia sighed and cursed.

"Are you saying that Jaylen's story is true?"

"Yes. They hacked his cellphone and computer and stole his ideas. Sold these to the highest bidder and then pretended to help him so that they can say that it's them guiding him."

"Bloody thieves!"

"Tell me about it. They are using a video-sender and sophisticated gadgets to hack, monitor and backtrack on people's activities. That could explain also why their project failed in the end. Jaylen accused them of stealing his ideas. He was adamant that they stole even with the mistakes he had made in his designs which he later proved was correct."

"We are talking about a sophisticated network that includes politicians, doctors and the so-called grassroots spies."

"So, it's also true that they tortured him to death to cover up for this."

"True. It's a billion-dollar scheme."

"That makes a lot of sense. I was wondering myself how these uneducated bastards end up that rich?"

"Bloody thieves, daylight robbers if you ask me."

"So, am I safe here?"

There was a moment of silence.

Miles away a door suddenly opened.

"We have a situation. There has been a security breach."

The man dressed in an expensive suit removed his suit jacket before sitting down. He looked calm and very relaxed.

"Nothing to worry about you know the protocol."

"Yes, Sir but..."

The man looked even more relaxed before breathing heavily.

"No buts just follow the procedure."

"I am afraid we cannot. One of us."

The man got up before walking to the window. He looked outside.

"What does he want?"

"I think curiosity got the better of him. Our grassroots spy."

"This can't get out otherwise we are finished."

"I know I will send my men straight away."

"Lone-wolf?"

The man walked to the window too and stood next to the man smartly dressed.

"Girlfriend, ours as well."

"I don't care you heard me. If this is out, we are all

finished."

"But Sir we never went for one of us."

"Are you hearing me? I am not taking any chances. Get rid of all."

There was silence in the room.

"She. I mean they are all also part of Directive 17?"

"Can that be fast forwarded?"

Jonathan was lying on the bed face up. His eyes moving fast beneath closed eyelids. He twitched his heard from left to right and back again. Instantly he snapped open the eyelids and looked around. He breathed heavily before sitting on the edge of the bed. He covered his face with his hands. He looked at the dressing table and reached for a picture frame. He looked at Karolina's picture. He looked in her eyes. He could see how it all started. That was the best time of his life he recalled. She was such a beauty full of confidence and charm. She was everything he wished for in a woman, beautiful, intelligent and charming. He loved her from the word go. He looked away for a while. He felt a lump choking him. Confusion was written all over his face. He knew Karolina was the only woman he wanted yet it seemed he is the one who had pushed her out of his life. He struggled to come to terms with the fact that she was someone's lover now. He quickly got up and walked to the study room. He retrieved his laptop and scrolled down documents. He got up and took his car keys and soon left the house. He opened the car glove compartment and retrieved a gun. He placed the gun on the passenger seat. His car overtook other cars leaving other drivers fuming with rage. He got out and entered the building. Up the stairs to the floors above. As soon as he had turned into the corridor a woman bumped into him causing her to drop her purse and touching his heart in the process. Jonathan knelt and picked up the purse and handed it to the woman without saying anything.

"Thank you." replied the woman looking at Jonathan.

He just lifted his eyebrows and continued through the corridor until he reached his office door. He entered inside and swiftly threw himself on the chair and searched inside the drawer. He took out the files that were inside and placed these on the desk. After a while he sighed and sat comfortably in the chair holding a file in his hand. He picked up the phone and dialed a number. Soon after he left the office.

At night a car entered a road to the suburbs. Inside was the excited Jonathan. He dialed a number while driving the car.

"Come on pick up the phone. Pick up the phone."

He said it loud looking ahead of the road with his car swerving left to right. The neighborhood was quiet, but street lights were still on.

"I just what to see the look in her eyes when I tell

this."

whispered Jonathan stepping on gas. The car drove for a while before coming to a halt outside a huge mansion. He quickly got out leaving the car door opened and ran toward the huge steel gates. A quick buzz on the telecommunication system outside but there was no reply. Nervously he paced outside the gate before pushing the huge gate. Surprisingly the gate was open. He stepped inside and instantly felt a sudden feeling of fear run down his spine. He instantly stopped and looked in front of him. He then proceeded inside the yard to the huge door. He shouted Karolina's name. He tried opening the door, but the door was locked. He walked away from the veranda and looked to the bedrooms on above levels expecting to see the lights being switched on. A sudden feeling of sadness struck him. Something was wrong. He looked around the property and noticed the 'For Sale' signs. He cursed and kicked hard the air. He quickly retrieved his cellphone and dialed. Instantly an automated voice greeted him. The number was no longer in use. A loud cry pierced the silent night waking up the neighbors who peered through the curtains.

CHAPTER FIVE

Karolina walked to the window of her office. She touched and rubbed her stomach and smiled before looking outside the window. A lot of things had happened. They had moved and relocated at the advice of Nick. Here and there she had thought about Jonathan especially now that she was pregnant. She had loved to get pregnant when she was with Jonathan but him being him he had postponed having kids early. She imagined what life could have been. Jonathan was a very loving family man whereas Nick was different, things had changed. The pressure to remain on top meant less quality time together. She sat down before a knock at the door startled her. Instantly before she had the chance to answer, the door swung wide open. It was Californika.

The two hooked up in each other's arms for a while.

"Yes. Looking good miss."

"Thanks. How has it been? You are not bad yourself."

"Been great. Just enjoying the best life has to offer you know with Tom it's live today like it's your last day."

"How is Tenerife?"

"Sunny and fabulous. You should visit us sometimes you and Nick. Leave the shop, come and see the other side of the world. I bet you will never want to return here. It's that beautiful you just want to enjoy this forever you know."

"Will see if Nick can agree to that."

"So, how is he?"

"Great! Just busy all the time now."

"So how is the new place?"

"Great even bigger and more luxurious than the previous one. Far away from Jonathan."

There was silence for a while. Californika got up and walked toward the window. She looked outside. She walked toward Karolina.

"Why you look like you have seen a ghost?"

"You said far away from Jonathan."

"Yes, I changed my number, I mean everything. He

was getting very agitated. I was scared you know. Nick was never home. He couldn't stop coming. At first it was okay until he started asking to move back in with me."

Californika looked at her friend.

"So, Nick asked you to move and change your number?"

"Yes."

"When was this?"

"Some months ago."

Californika sat next to her friend and hugged her tightly.

"He shot himself. He is dead. Jonathan is dead."

A loud cry pierced the office building.

The two women wept profusely.

"I had no idea that he is dead."

"I know. It's okay. He was tormented. There is nothing you could have done."

"I never wished him dead even though he was a pain."

"It's okay. I know you loved each other. Sometimes just the way things are."

"I never thought he could kill himself."

There was silence.

Californika opened her purse and took out a clean handkerchief and wiped her tears.

"Even now I thought Nick had something to do with this."

Karolina glanced at Californika with piercing eyes.

"No! Nick. No! He is a good man."

"Exactly! You complained Jonathan was becoming a pain, so he had to do something."

Karolina quickly got up and walked to the window and looked outside. She turned and looked at Californika.

"No. I never wished him dead. I love him..."

She broke down and cried.

"I loved him. He pushed me away."

She cried profusely.

"So how is Nick?"

Karolina blew her nose.

"That could explain everything."

"What do you mean?"

"He has been cold lately. He must have felt really bad about all this."

"Are you sure he has nothing to do with this?"

"What makes you even suggest something like this?"

"I don't know. When things like this happen after the

fracas it's easy to think that way."

"He is a good man and will never go to that extent."

"Maybe because he loved you. Especially when you got pregnant. Some people go to extremes to protect their loved ones."

Karolina sighed and sat down.

Days later a convertible car drove slowly down the road until it came to a sudden halt beside the road. Inside was a woman with a cloth covering her hair and sunglasses. She sat in the car for a while before finding the strength to open the door. She was sobbing. Her long dress danced to the wind even though the sun was high up. She walked to a house and stood outside. She looked around as if lost. She retrieved keys from her purse and entered the deserted house. The woman was Karolina who was pregnant. She stood in the lounge area and memories brought down more tears. She remembered the first time they met. She never thought of loving another. Jonathan was her ideal-man even though she- wished he could do better. They talked about starting their own business. Jonathan was a very cautious person. He wanted and trusted things he had tried. A business, according to him carried more risks and above all he never wanted to venture into new territory. She walked nervously toward the bedroom expecting to see Jonathan in there somehow. Nervously she entered the bedroom. She wept hard and lay on the bed. After a while she got up and searched his house for anything. She opened his laptop and went through it. She stopped and glanced at her photo with Jonathan on the dressing table. She felt having difficulties breathing. She still loved him. She checked the last person dialed the night he died. Instantly she started sobbing even more profusely. She felt sorry for him that she sat down.

"Oh, Jonathan you didn't have to kill yourself. Why? First you walk away from me even though I loved you and now you have gone out of my life forever. Why?"

She sobbed uncontrollably.

"Is that how you love someone? Tell me Jonathan? Is that?"

She threw herself onto the bed and cried.

Later she collected his laptop and headed to the city. She went and took his autopsy report before heading home. Nick was not home the time she arrived. She headed upstairs and took a long bath. The barking of the dog woke her up. After a while she heard the front doors opening.

"Darling I am home." shouted Nick running upstairs.

He pushed open the bedroom door, and the bedroom was empty. He rushed to the bathroom and entered the unlocked door.

"I love you so much. Never leave me. Okay?" whispered Nick passionately kissing Karolina.

"Where would I go?"

"I don't know. I am just saying that we should be together you know. Especially now that we have a baby coming our way."

"I love you."

"I know I love you too. Very much. In fact. Karolina, I love you more."

Instantly Karolina burst into tears and cried profusely to Nick's surprise.

"What did I say? Did I say something wrong my darling?"

"No. It's just I love you and don't want to lose you."

Nick looked confused for a while.

"You don't need to cry for that. You know I love you and will always do. I don't know what I will do to anyone who will try to stop us."

Karolina sobbed and looked at Nick with piercing eyes.

"Even Jonathan?"

"Especially that bastard. I nearly killed that prick. Was he here? What is wrong my love you look shaken? What is happening my love tell me?"

Instantly Karolina wore a confused look.

"You don't know?"

"Know what?"

Karolina started sobbing.

Nick hugged her and kissed her all over.

"Jonathan died months ago."

The couple looked at each other speechless.

"He died. How did he die?" asked Nick softly not expecting an answer. He sighed heavily and hugged Karolina tighter.

A strange feeling struck Karolina.

She looked like she had seen a ghost. Nick was so calm and emotionless. Surely, she had expected some sorrow on his part after all they had spent time together even if it was just arguing that must have enticed a reaction from him.

"I thought you knew."

Nick sighed.

"Not really. I didn't know he was dead."

"You don't have to lie to me."

"It's the truth. You believe me, right?"

Karolina looked at Nick.

"Makes no sense unless if you knew he was dead?"

"Then ask us to move and change your number? Why?"

"So that I won't know that he is dead."

"Darling what makes you even say that? I didn't like

the guy but to kill him is something else."

"But you just said that you would kill anyone who stresses me out?"

"I know but killing him..."

Nick got up and sighed heavily.

"You have to trust me on this one. I didn't kill him. He must have shot himself."

"Okay, I apologize. I believe you my love. I love you more. Never leave me okay. Promise."

Nick passionately hugged Karolina and kissed her continuously.

"You are my life now. I love you."

The couple hugged each other before passionately making love.

In the morning Karolina could hear Nick's heart beat beating normally as she lay on top of him with her head on his chest. Instantly the heart beat disappeared. Instantly her eyelids snapped open. She looked at his hairy chest before raising her head. She looked at him lying peacefully on the bed. A closer look at his eyes revealed eyes moving fast beneath closed eyelids. She had seen him like this before. An instant feeling of fear struck her, and she froze in front of him. Instantly he opened his eyes. Karolina opened wide her eyes in shock and fear, as soon as their eyes met. He smiled but quickly wore a troubled look.

"Hey darling good morning."

Karolina did not reply but instead stared at him before looking at his chest. He looked surprised as well. In turn he looked at Karolina before staring at his chest and then back at Karolina.

"Are you sure you are okay?"

"I am darling. Good morning to you my love."

She lay over him and kissed him passionately.

"I want right now. Let's just stay home today."

"Hm. I love you and would love to, but you know I have to go."

"Get someone to cover for you. I need you. Just want to be with you my love."

"I know. Me too but..."

Karolina stubbed Nick with her tongue and the couple hooked in each other's arms. They made passionate love. A few minutes later Karolina slumped on the bed next to him.

"Just can't seem to get enough of you."

"You know what? I can cancel my appointments for this morning and spend some quality time with you?"

"Sounds good darling."

"But just for this morning. I will come back early tonight. Then take the rest of the week off what do you say darling."

Karolina hugged him before the couple started kissing again. She knelt on the bed and placed her head flat down on the bed before closing her yes.

Later that afternoon she opened her eyes and moved her hand all over the bed.

"Nick."

She whispered his name, but he had already gone.

She lay on the bed for a while. Instantly a strange feeling struck her. She quickly got up and retrieved the telephone records for the previous months. She scrolled down on the laptop. She stopped and placed the laptop down. She left the bedroom but returned after a few minutes. She sat down and looked at the documents in her hands. She took the laptop again and looked at the telephone records for the previous address. She slumped back.

"Oh my God!"

She retrieved Jonathan's autopsy report and looked at the report. She looked at the telephone report. Instantly she picked up everything and headed out of the house before driving away.

Months back.

A car parked outside Jonathan's house. Jonathan got out leaving the car door open and staggered inside the house. Soon afterward he walked out and entered the car before driving off. He drove the car to the city center. He parked the car and staggered toward the city center. He stopped and thought for a while then resumed walking. He passed a fountain in the park in the middle of the city before something startled him. His heart beat rose exponentially that he touched his heart. Instantly he had a flash back when someone bumped into him. He recalled the place when that had happened and started tracing his movement of that day. That took him to the heart of the city. He stopped and looked around. There was a bank in front of him. He had been to this bank that morning depositing money as part of his job. Further down was the insurance company. He turned around and looked to the other sides. There were beautician shops and other small shops. He stopped and thought for a while. Nothing seemed to make sense. He walked toward the route he had taken that morning when instantly he felt like bumping into someone. He stopped and looked around before touching his heart. He looked around and in front of him was a huge building. The sign was written; TWO, with a victory hand sign. As soon as he had passed the place which a man bumped into him some months before he felt a strange feeling and pain before he fell to the ground. When he got up he was disoriented for a while. He walked back to his car and sat down before driving back home. Later that evening Jonathan entered his house and sat down in the sitting room. He felt a huge lump in his chest and was about to burst into tears when he staggered into the study room. He opened the drawer and saw a gun. He picked the gun and pointed the gun on himself. He aimed the gun at his forehead but suddenly moved the gun to his heart.

"You stole my love. The only woman I loved. I know you don't love her but there is one way she will find out."

He looked at Karolina's photo on the desk and instantly stopped. He cried forcibly trying not to make any noise. Mucus trickled down across his lips before he wiped it off. He retrieved his cellphone and dialed Karolina's phone number, but the number was no longer in use. He dialed her house number and Nick picked up the phone.

"Who is this?" asked Nick as the voice patterns revealed a troubled man on the other end.

"You, bastard. You think you are clever. But I am going to show you that the woman is mine. If you don't believe me, wait you will find out soon. She will see you for what you really are. A petty thief stealing my love for her. You think you can love her forever."

Nick interrupted instantly.

"Hold on. I don't have time for all this nonsense. Don't call again. Okay."

"You think I am bluffing. After tonight she will find out the truth. I am going to put a big hole in that love of yours."

He started laughing sarcastically louder and louder.

"You are not good for her. You lied. We both know

the truth. Guess what? We met months before you started seeing her. Outside the bank in the city. Remember?"

"Are you fucking drunk or what? I don't know what you are talking about."

Jonathan couldn't stop laughing.

"You thought you are clever but wait and see what I have in store for you."

"Don't do anything stupid. Jonathan!"

"Now I got your attention. I will be man enough and give you a choice. Walk away if you really love her or let her watch you die tonight. If I were you, I would walk away. If you really love her. Don't let her watch this."

"What are you talking about? Are you fucking out of your mind?"

"Five past two."

"What five past two?"

There was silence for a while.

"I give you until two o'clock in the morning to leave her. Walk away. If you are still with her by two o'clock she will witness, you die."

"You come here I will shoot you myself. I am not playing games. I think you have a death wish."

Jonathan remained silent for a while.

"You bastard admit you stole my love for her."

"Are you mad? How did I do that?"

There was silence.

In a cool and calculated voice replied Jonathan.

"You touched my heart."

"What? Where? So, what?"

"Say goodbye to Karolina for me."

Instantly the line went dead.

Nick walked up and down before Karolina's voice startled him.

"Who is it darling is everything okay?"

Nick ran upstairs and entered the bedroom. Karolina was sitting on the bed with a laptop in her hands doing her work.

"The business is doing great. I need to spend more time at work until after the promotional campaign darling."

Nick felt relieved that Karolina didn't insist to know who had phoned.

"Great! That's okay with me."

Karolina looked surprised.

"Are you sure you are okay?"

"Yes, darling just tired and I want to call in early."

"Who was on the phone?"

"My friend from work he wants me to go to his party until two in the morning."

"Don't stop on my account. I am busy anyway."

"Just want to spend some quality time with you."

"Oh, you are sweet. I love you, you know."

"I love you too. In fact, I love you more."

Nick jumped on the bed and kissed Karolina passionately. He hugged her very tight not letting go.

"Nick." whispered Karolina trying to loosen Nick's grip.

"Oh sorry."

"Are you sure you are okay? Okay come."

Karolina placed the laptop away and lay down on top of Nick. After a while she stopped rubbing her body onto his and looked at him.

"Darling are you sure you are okay."

Nick looked surprised.

"Why are you asking?"

Instantly he got the idea.

"I apologize junior is miles away too. Come he must be warm now."

They both started laughing.

Miles away Jonathan got up and entered the bedroom. He sat on the bed and retrieved his photo with

Karolina. He cried profusely before looking at the table clock. He entered the study room and sat on the desk. He relived his time with Karolina. The first time they met and all those mornings she woke up next to him. He realized that he was very lucky. At the same time, he just knew that no other woman will ever love him the way she loved him. He closed his eyes and aimed at his chest before a gunshot sound rocketed in the skies.

Karolina opened Jonathan's house door and entered inside. She went into the study room and switched the computer on before going through Jonathan's documents. She got up and went in the lounge area. She stood near the window and looked outside. They had stayed together in this house. There were a lot of memories that she found it hard to control her tears. She flipped open the curtain and looked outside. The protruding letters in the letter box outside caught her attention. She walked outside and took all the letters into the house. She checked all, and one letter caught her attention. She had seen a similar logo before. She turned around the letter before quickly opening it. She entered the house and researched about this company. The search results yielded a lot of outcomes and only two caught her attention. The first one was a political party called TWO led by a one David. She went through the website and there was no link whatsoever to what was in the letter. The other one was a small company somewhere in Latvia proposing to make people very rich and offering help in managing people's finances. She scrolled through the internet search results and retrieved a phone number. She sat down and dialed. The phone rung for a while before an automated voice answered the call. The automated voice requested her that she entered the country code from which she was calling from. As soon as she had dialed the codes, the call was diverted back to the USA.

The phone rung for a while before a woman answered the phone.

"Where are your offices if I can ask?"

"Here in the USA Headquarters in New York city."

She relaxed as soon as she heard this.

"Is this a bank?"

"Yes, we deal with insurances as well."

"Car insurances?"

"Yes, all kinds of insurances."

Karolina placed down the phone and huffed.

The ringing of her cellphone startled her.

"Hi darling. I am on my way back home. See you soon."

She took Jonathan's letters and downloaded some documents to an external drive and left.

On her way back home, a lot of questions were

running through her head.

Nick was in the lounge when the door suddenly opened. Excited to see Karolina he got up and walked fast to her before holding her in his arms. He kissed her passionately all over.

"I thought that maybe you left me. Trust me, I don't want to feel like that ever again."

"No darling I just went for a walk I did not know what time you were going to come back."

"Let's just say I am very happy to see you."

He knelt and kissed her stomach at the same time listening to it.

"I think he will be a boy."

"A big boy. I feel heavy already."

"Come my darling you sit here and relax okay."

Karolina dropped her hand bag on the carpet something she never did before. The bag made a loud sound that startled Nick.

"Hey what's in there. Stones or what?"

They both laughed as Nick tried to pick the hand bag up.

"No Darling. Leave the bag there. I will need some items inside after I have relaxed."

Nick first checked the weight. The bag was heavy and puffed. He simply looked at Karolina before going to the bedroom.

She waited to hear him open the bedroom door before she picked up the laptop and started scrolling. Quickly she entered some information and scrolled looking for anything. Her heart beat beating faster with every minute she accessed Nick's documents and paused for a while looking to the passage to the bedroom. One click, and the document opened and instantly Nick appeared on the stairs. The look on her face sends signals to Nick. He instantly knew that she was up to something, but he played it cool. He walked behind her and quickly she closed the lid of the laptop and the couple started kissing passionately.

"I have been longing for you all day you know darling?"

Yeah that's my lady. That's what I want to hear. I love you. I can't wait for you to give birth. If it's a boy, we will call him Nick junior.

"What if it's a girl?"

"I don't think so. The way the pregnancy is growing, it must be a big boy."

"I agree but I am just saying that what if it's a big girl?"

"Name her after me."

"Perfect."

The sense of fear and curiosity heightened Karolina's feelings that she trembled with lust and cravings. This was not new to her because of her pregnancy. She wanted Nick close to her. She wanted to hug him and let him squeeze her all over. That night they made love all night. She knew she had to wear him off before she can venture back looking for clues. Jonathan had claimed that Nick was not true to her. Maybe he was right after all. She trusted him but still this nagging feeling wouldn't go away.

"You make me feel like a teenager on heat."

"We should be together forever."

"Never leave me. I am all yours. All this is yours. If that keeps us together so be it. I don't want to lose you my love."

"I don't know what I will do without you."

"Come I will make love to you like it's our first time."

"Hold me tight darling."

The couple kissed passionately snogging most of the night. The last time she gave an intense orgasm Karolina fell asleep. Nick tried to wake her up, but she was in a deep sleep. He hugged her and put his leg over her and fell asleep too.

Karolina woke up and crept away from the sleeping Nick. She stealthily tip-toed to the lounge area. She sat down and took the laptop. She continued checking. She opened one document in Nick's folder that caught her attention.

She stopped and placed the laptop down. She took

her hand bag and opened inside. She retrieved the external drive she had saved some documents from Jonathan's computer. She scrolled down the documents. She found documents both from the TWO insurance company. A company based somewhere in the Baltic countries purporting to help people manage their monies and make them rich. The one thing that caught her attention was the identical reference numbers. What were the chances that Nick, and Jonathan had reference numbers that were in chronological sequence? She stopped as her heart beat elevated significantly.

She searched all the documents using this reference number. A huge list came up. She then arranged the documents in order the oldest first.

She clicked open the first document. She was gob smacked.

It was a no strings attached cash deposit of $1 million that can be repaid back as a loan throughout one's life. All Nick had to do was to tick a box and confirm. She stopped and looked upstairs and listened. The house was silent. Curiosity killed her.

"Did Nick accepted the money?" she whispered quickly going through the account's documents.

She stopped and breathed heavily.

"Damn!" she whispered.

Her heart started beating very fast.

She looked at the screen thinking before she continued scrolling the documents.

On the external drive she noticed a document that caught her attention. Five months before she split up with Jonathan, his car insurance's monthly payments had tripled. She stopped and recalled. Jonathan did not change his car since the time they met she thought. The time they met he had just got a new car. Since then his insurance should have gone down over the years as he was a good driver. She looked for any documents from this TWO company but there were none.

She stopped and thought for a while.

She scrolled back on Nick's documents. She stopped and looked shocked. Quickly she retrieved Jonathan's autopsy report and looked at it. Instantly Nick's voice startled her that she peed herself.

"What are you doing down here? Come let's go and sleep darling."

She pushed the laptop closed and followed Nick upstairs. She could feel the small droplets of urine trickling down her legs.

Nick stopped and looked at her.

"Are you okay my love?"

"Only if you knew what pregnant women go through."

"Doing a great job. Bringing angels into this world."

He turned around and hugged her kissing her passionately.

"I love you. There is so many things I want to talk to you about, but I just can't seem to find the right time."

Karolina's heart beat shot up instantly. She simply opened wide her eyes and stared at Nick.

"Do you love me and the baby?"

Nick looked confused for a while.

"What?"

He looked at her.

"What makes you ask that?"

She looked down.

"Nothing. I am just asking."

That night a cool shiver ran down her spine. Nick spooned her and hugged her tightly kissing her back passionately before the couple fell asleep.

Early morning as soon as Nick had left for work a car screeched to a halt outside the mansion. She opened the gates and Californika walked into the yard walking as fast as she can.

A quick loud knock at the door and she entered inside.

Karolina ran downstairs as soon as she heard Californika shouting her name.

The two women hugged each other. They both started crying.

"What's wrong Karo."

"I don't know. I don't know what to believe now."

"What happened?"

She sobbed uncontrollably.

"I don't know if I know this Nick anymore."

"Off course he is your lover. You are expecting a beautiful baby together. Nothing to worry about. He is rich and handsome. Man, like that don't come easily."

"That's exactly what is worrying me."

"What? Get real? What's wrong with a rich man?"

"I am not sure if he got rich the right way."

"What really are you saying? My friend."

She sobbed for a while.

"I just found out that he received a lump sum money few days after Jonathan's death."

"Coincidence! Heard of that word before? I thought you said he has his own businesses?"

She sobbed further.

"Thought so. Maybe a bounty hunter. Or soul collector,"

"What?"

"Insurance-soul collector."

"Never heard of such a thing."

She sobbed looking at her stomach.

"I am pregnant? I don't know why this is happening."

"Still waiting to hear about the insurance-soul collector term."

"It's a long story. There is this company called TWO in Baltic countries. I guess they hack into everyone's cellphone, computer and television and generate a profile of your habits. They look at your income and expenditure. I mean everything. They look at if you have a life insurance cover. If not but you are in the perfect group. They arrange one behind your back and assign a catalyst?"

"Catalyst?"

"Yes, you know to speed up everything. The assassin if you like."

"Damn! Are those rumors for real?"

"I just don't know how I ended up into all this?"

There was a moment of silence.

"Like I was saying. This Catalyst, the Assassin gets a huge cash advance in $ millions. The money is deposited into his account. All he has to do is tick a box and confirm."

"That's it?"

"Just like that and you are a millionaire?"

"Just like that. Then you must replace the other person."

"The one they will arrange a life insurance behind his back?"

"Correct."

"Wait a minute do you mean Jonathan?"

Karolina looked at Californika without a word.

"Holy Sugar!"

She stood up and walked around.

"You have to go to the police or something."

"Hello!" she pointed at her pregnant stomach.

"So, are you saying that people in Baltic countries arrange this? Start making sense. Okay?"

"I found out last night that Nick received a lump sum days after Jonathan's death. The money was from a local bank."

"So, are you saying that he knew Jonathan was dead even before he asked you to relocate? I think he used some money to buy this house.?"

Karolina started sobbing.

"He was telling the truth after all."

Californika stood up and walked around the lounge area.

"So, what do you suggest? Did he change? Does he know you know?"

"That's the confusing bit. He has changed for the better. He has never showed me this kind of love. We made love last night like never. He kissed me passionately and hugged me all night before that it was just a good night and a kiss that's it."

"Hmm. Okay. Does he know? Did he suspect?"

"Not really."

"Either we go to the police or."

"Or what?"

CHAPTER SIX

Nick got out of this new limousine he had just bought. He stood still and straightened his suit jacket. He then corrected the position of his tie. Soon after he moistened his sleek hair with the saliva on the tip of his fingers. He looked a million dollars and walked likewise. Everyone cheered and applauded as he entered the building in the city. There was a business meeting of all international businessmen. His businesses had flourished for the past months. Angela walked toward him. She was dressed-to-kill. She had shining and sleek long blond hair with a smile that was so cute that made one always smile back. She walked like a model in high heels as she approached to welcome Nick. Nick stopped for a while and looked everywhere before staring at Angela. He looked at his ring and lifted his lips like a fish before hugging Angela. The pair walked into the building before disappearing.

"You look fabulous tonight. If it wasn't for this surely tonight, I could have said come back in the limousine with me." said Nick flashing the ring.

"Oh, thank you. You are not bad yourself, Sir. By the way, you can wear another one. One for me."

"You are right I never thought it that way."

The pair laughed before entering the conference room. A beep sound from his pager went off instantaneously. Nick looked at his guests before retrieving his pager. A message was on the pager's screen.

'$5 million dollars has been transferred to your account. Tick the box to accept and confirm or decline the offer.'

Nick looked confused but curious. Damn he felt like a king. The thoughts of Jonathan quickly erased the happiness from his face. He looked at Angela.

He felt excited. Over the past months he had felt really attracted to her even though he was now married to Karolina. She was every men's dream. She knew how to bring out the best in men. I guess some people are just like that.

"$5 million dollars and all that!" he grinned with joy.

"I promise this will be my last job. I will have a baby to look after soon," he whispered to himself.

He imagined what Angela's boyfriend was like. Surely, he must have been rich he thought.

"$5 million dollars?" he whispered to himself.

Throughout the speech he couldn't take his eyes off Angela. He knew this was a big catch. After the conference he didn't waste time. He walked toward Angela with much confidence now than before. He could see more than the $5 million in his account. That body was hitting all the right knots. Surely somehow her body was calling him or, so he thought. He just walked to her and grabbed her by the waist holding her very tight close to himself and gently kissed her on her side cheek next to her lips. Firmly he held her hand and pulled her toward himself. Up close, he looked at her. He realized that she was more beautiful than he had thought. He could see her beautiful eyes glittering with surprise and lust. He did not say anything but leaned very close and gave her a smacker. She in turn passionately closed her eyes before kissing him back.

"Sir, I think here it might not be a good idea."

"Good idea to who?"

In his mind he would do anything for the $5 million. She was worth more to him now than before.

Outside, the limousine's windows rolled up before smoothly leaving the city heading to the suburb area. The pair started snogging passionately.

"Hold on."

Nick flattened the limousine's seat until there was a bed.

He unfastened Angela's trousers belt and pulled off the trouser as she lifted her legs up to reveal probably one of Carolinadeivid's sexy white lingerie range. Instantly the music started playing and the limousine's lights change to a dark red theme giving the inside the romantic feel. The limousine cruised out of the city. Angela got up and wiped herself between her legs using her knickers and slid the knickers into Nick's suit jacket before kissing him passionately.

"I will drop you off. We meet again at the next conference. Okay?"

"Okay, Sir."

"Call me Nick."

"Okay, Nick." she kissed him passionately.

The limousine came to a smooth stop, and the door opened. Angela got off and looked at Nick as the limousine's window slid down. She started walking toward a house as the window slowly closed. The limousine smoothly cruised away.

Nick opened the mansion door and stealthily walked in. He had seen that the bedroom light was still on. He walked into the bedroom. Karolina was fast asleep. He breathed heavily. Quickly he walked out of the bedroom and into the bathroom. He took a quick shower. Back in the bedroom Karolina cried secretly.

After taking the shower Nick entered the study room and dialed Angela's cellphone.

Instantly she picked up the cellphone.

"Been a great night hope we can do this again soon."

"Can you? What about your?"

Nick quickly interrupted.

"Don't worry about her."

"If you say so. Nick."

"Who are you talking to this time?" asked Karolina standing at the door.

Nick's heart split into two.

"Oh my God! You startled me. No one! Just my limousine driver."

"Where were you until this time?"

"Darling we had a conference meeting at work. I told you. I apologize for after the conference I went with my friends. You know what? Things are going to be perfect forever. I am going to sell part of my business. We will have extra money soon. I will have all the time in the world to us. Just you and me and our baby off course."

"How much are you going to get after the sale?" asked Karolina.

"$5 million dollars."

That week Nick was the happiest man on earth. He could not wait for Friday to arrive. Friday was a blessed day to him. He had planned to tick the box and confirm as instructed. This was serious money to mess about. He had sworn that this was the last time he was going to be a catalyst or an assassin. He wanted a normal life like everyone else. Karolina being pregnant meant more to him than money.

"I love you very much."

Karolina for the first time did not reply but instead looked at Nick with her shining blue eyes piercing at him. Only if eyes could kill.

"You don't have to worry anymore. This Friday I will put everything right. I am going to prove to you that I love you and want to be with you for the sake of our son or daughter."

"I will just have to wait and see."

Friday was like no other Friday. Nick was never this excited as far as Karolina can remember. He had made passionate love to Karolina every morning and evening that week except this Friday morning. His thoughts were somewhere else. He just got up and went straight to the bathroom. He shaved like a model going on show. He wore his most expensive aftershave and his best suit. He had trimmed and done his hair. He stood in front of the bedroom wall mirror and smiled.

"How do I look?"

Jealous was setting Karolina on fire especially the fact that he had skipped his morning glory with her. She knew he was going to fuck Angela instead. Strong feelings of being used and neglected now that she was pregnant choked her that she couldn't breathe for a while.

"Yes. What do you say my love?"

"Perfect."

"That's my lady there," he pointed at Karolina's image in the mirror. She sat on the bed for a while whilst he dressed up and admired himself.

She stood up and walked toward him. She stumbled for a while trying to get Nick's attention but just a reflex he waited until she was close to him.

"The baby is growing fast. I feel bad going and leaving you alone like this. Maybe I should cancel the meeting and spend some quality time with you. What do you say?"

Karolina hold back the tears. Nick could see her blue eyes glittering with tears.

"Nothing to worry about. I will be back before you know it. I love you and the baby."

The couple hugged and snogged. Soon afterward Karolina stormed out of the bedroom. Nick stood there admiring himself by the time it sunk in Karolina was already coming back to the bedroom. Instantly as Nick left the bedroom Karolina bumped into him at the bedroom door and touched his heart.

He looked shocked, surprised and confused. He had this sense of fear which was written all over his face. He looked like he had seen a ghost. He just couldn't believe what had just happened. He tried pushing the thought aside, but Karolina cunningly smiled as she quickly sped away. He stood there for a while not knowing what to say or do. He had seen that cunning smile before. It was a cunning smile of victory. In fact, that was his trade mark smile after what he called the kill. He knew that that smile haunted one to the grave. He stood there speechless. Instantly his heart nearly exploded as it started beating very fast. He found himself having trouble breathing. He unfastened his tie grip and sighed heavily.

"$5 million." he whispered softly.

He walked downstairs after Karolina. In her night dress she walked downstairs without any shoes in her legs, with her night dress dancing to her movements. It seemed as if it was all happening in slow motion to him. He could see her long blonde curls floating in the air as she walked downstairs frequently looking back at him and smiling. As soon as she had reached the bottom stairs, she stopped and looked at him. She flipped her dress up and slowly removed her knickers. Briefly he stopped on the stairs and looked at her. He continued until he reached where she was. He leaned on her as she stood there with her knickers in her hand. He slowly kissed her. She passionately kissed him protracting her tongue fully into his mouth and holding his head messing his sleek combed hair. She pushed him before she knelt to unzip his trousers. Instantly a quick and loud knock at the door startled both. He tried to open the door, but she slumped against the door shutting it back.

"Fuck me! Fuck me now. Let her hear everything too. Come fuck me Nick."

She gave him her back pulling her night dress up before she leaned against the door.

"Give me back. Fuck me. Keep her waiting. Let her listen to everything behind the closed door."

Nick tried but somehow, he just couldn't.

"I have to go darling."

"Fuck me Nick. Let her hear everything too."

"I have to go. I love you. See you tonight."

"What? Am I not attractive to you anymore is that so?" she whispered.

Instantly she turned to face him and kneed him in the groin.

He growled in pain.

Angela hearing Nick's growls instantly knocked at the door.

Karolina opened the door.

She pulled her night dress down. Angela stared and

saw Nick closing his zip. She looked in Karolina's hand and saw her holding her knickers. Nick tried to cover up for the pain from being kneed in the groin that he smiled at Angela. Her face creased for a while with rage. Karolina walked closer to Angela and touched her lips before letting her smell her knickers. She shoved them in her suit jacket.

"Darling I am going. See you tonight."

Karolina's eyes had turned to red with rage and jealous.

"You stole my heart. You stole my love. You are nothing than just a heart-thief."

Nick froze on hearing that. These were Jonathan's words.

Fear crippled him for a while. He stood there speechless. It was like a nightmare to him. He just couldn't believe that this was happening.

"What did you say?"

"Oh, just a minute I have a present from your twin."

"My twin?"

Nick looked at Angela surprised and confused at the same time.

Karolina ran back into the mansion. They both could hear her footsteps going up.

"Be careful you don't want to fall and injure my baby."

Soon after the door opened.

Karolina handed a gun to Nick.

"Your twin brother said that you can have this as you will need it."

Nick looked shocked and surprised.

"Darling I have bodyguards no need to carry a gun,"

Karolina laughed sarcastically.

"I am just saying if you can't fuck her with your dick maybe use this."

She smiled cunningly and flashed her hairy pussy at her.

"Oho! What got into her today?"

"I don't know. Pregnancy hormones playing tricks on her. Been very jealous lately."

"Should we not be going now?"

"I love you see you tonight."

Nick and Angela started walking away toward the limousine. Nick was about to enter the limousine when Karolina shouted at him.

He stopped and turned around.

"What is it my love?"

"Oh, by the way I ticked the box for you and confirmed." She winked instantly. Angela on seeing this looked at Nick.

"What is she talking about?"

Nick's heart felt like it had split into two.

"She stole my love. She is nothing but a heart-thief,"

Karolina laughed pointing at Angela.

Instantly she stopped laughing.

"You don't love me. You don't care about us, about my baby. You would rather fuck her. If you really love me, love us, me and the baby then you will know what to do."

Karolina touched her stomach and entered inside the mansion. She waited behind the door crying hoping Nick would cancel the meeting but the sound of the limousine driving away tore her heart apart. She opened the door and saw Nick looking back at her as the limousine drove off. Inside the limousine he quickly opened the laptop and checked his bank account. Surely the money was in the account he shared with Karolina. That meant that she had ticked the box and confirmed.

"Wow $5 million dollars?" whispered Angela.

Nick forced a smile.

Angela took the laptop and put it away.

"I know what you need. Flatten the seats. I will give you. I know you want me. He looked into her blue eyes and felt blood running down very fast. Quickly she unfastened her suit trousers, and she was not wearing any knickers. She pulled him to the flattened seats and pushed him down before jumping on him.

"Oh, he growled in pain. Your leg on junior."

"Oh sorry." she whispered quickly unfastening his trousers.

"Wait, a minute. What did your boyfriend say last time? What's his name again? What does he do? Where does he work?"

"Too many questions. Not the right time."

Instantly the music started playing. The driver of the limousine smiled as the limousine headed to the city center.

A lot of questions where running in his head.

Who was his target? Was the contract in his name? How did Karolina know about the money? Why she gave him the gun? Why was she acting strange? And above all this why re-enact Jonathan? Why did she give Angela her knickers?

Angela did not give him any time to think she rode him hard and fast. He had been going through mixed feelings. Fear and extreme excitement alternating. He looked at Angela as he came hard before growling. A knock on the glass that separates the driver and the back of the limousine startled both. Angela slumped on top of him and started laughing.

"I can do this forever with you. Take me to heaven again and back."

She started laughing.

"I think even with my ex-boyfriend I never experienced such intense orgasm."

For the first time Nick smiled genuinely. That's all he wanted to hear. She got up and looked around. She retrieved her suit jacket and took his wife's knickers and wore them. Nick looked at her, but his mind was miles away.

"Hey, are those my wife's knickers?"

"I gave her mine last week."

She raised her eyebrows.

Nick fumed with rage.

"How could you do this to me? Now I know why she has been acting strange,"

"I will do anything for $5 million."

"What? Did I mention something to do with the money last week?"

Nick looked confused and unsure.

"No, you did not but my girlfriend told me."

"What?"

Angela laughed.

"OK remember you asked me who my boyfriend was. What he did and his name?"

"Yes."

"I am in love with Karo."

Nick got up and wore his trousers before sitting up.

"What?"

"Yes. I love her."

"Which Karo. My Karo?"

"No! My Karolina."

Angela opened the door and got out. A lot of people had gathered outside the building. She looked around before looking at Nick. He got out of the limousine.

"You stole my love. You are nothing than a heart-thief."

Nick raised his head and looked at Angela. She in turn pointed in the crowd. A quick glance in the crowd before another long look at Angela. Instantly he jerked backward then again and again before leaning onto the limousine.

"Californika. Why?"

Californika walked toward him and leaned next to him.

He smiled.

"Californika. Very predictable."

He coughed blood holding his shoulder. He smiled again.

"Search in my pocket quickly."

Californika searched quickly first retrieving some

white knickers. He looked at her and then at the panties.

"Where did those came from?"

"No, search again."

This time she retrieved a note.

"Promise our secret."

Californika read the note. She closed her eyes and hold the gun to the side of her head.

"Do it?"

"You bastard! Why don't you be a man like Jonathan and do it yourself? Oh my God I cannot do it?"

Nick laughed.

"What is so funny?"

"I shot that bastard in cold blood. He begged for his life."

"What?"

"Yes that's right?"

"I introduced him to Jesus you coward!"

A bullet sound rocketed into the skies and everyone took cover.

She continued reading the note before a scream sent everyone ducking.

"He set me up!"

Angela knelt to pick up the note and it read:

"I know that only you love Karolina more than me. The love I had for her was borrowed love. To put it in Jonathan's terms I am nothing than just a heart-thief. This was my job until I met Karolina. I never thought love could look me in the eye. I had a contract to kill all and trade you for insurance money. Trophy hunters live by their rules, but that thing called love replaced rules with emotions. Rationality out of the window. I felt like a kid. She made me feel like a kid inside. I was an insurance-soul hunter working on commission until I met Karo. I am sorry for Jonathan, but he killed himself. I understand why now. I would rather die than not love her again. It's funny somehow that she stole my love for her this morning the moment she touched my heart. I felt like there is no tomorrow without her. When Angela told me that she was in love with Karo. I knew that was the end of me. I would rather die than not to love her again. I would rather die than to kill her above all she is carrying my beautiful handsome son or gorgeous daughter. Tell her I love her. New-life erased past sins. They will never send another assassin you should be safe now. I know you love her, and you will take care of her and my kid. Postscript [PS] tell my kid I love him or her or very much."

Californika sobbed uncontrollably. The background music coming from the limousine was the Elinadeivid song Trophy Hunters.

Trophy hunters live by their rules.

I was a trophy hunter not until I met love.

Never thought love could look me in the eyes.

Trophy is their slogan.

Trophy hunter bring me trophy

Trophy hunter bring me love.

CHAPTER SEVEN

Its Twins!!

Karolina was giving birth in the hospital. She had been screaming for a while now. Californika and Angela were on her bedside. They were comforting her as the labor contractions got more and more frequent. Californika held her leg and stroked it gently.

"Push! Come on push Karolina," urged Californika.

Angela had a wet cloth dozing Karolina's forehead.

The midwife touched her stomach before urging her to push as well.

Karolina took a long breath before spreading her legs apart and pushing continuously breathing-in in between. She screamed in agony.

"Breathe in. Breathe in. Then try again."

Karolina looked exhausted but determined to give birth. Angela knelt next to her. She looked at her in her eyes and kissed her.

"I know you can do it."

"I can't it hurts. I just can't."

"Push okay keep on pushing."

"I can see the head. I can see the head," said the midwife.

Californika looked at Angela and both the women looked at each other happily.

"Push. Keep pushing."

The midwife looked between Karolina's legs and quickly pulled the head of the baby and then quickly grabbed the placenta cord. Karolina screamed in agony. Californika and Angela looked at Karolina but excited that the baby was out. The midwife was busy pulling the rest of the baby's body. Karolina screamed in agony and pushed as hard as she can before slumping back on the bed. The midwife quickly clipped the placenta cord and checked the baby. The other ladies were very happy. The midwife after cleaning the baby was about to give the baby to Californika.

"Let me hold my baby." said Karolina.

"What about the other? We need to deliver the other." said the midwife.

"What?"

All the three ladies looked at each other.

"Twins!"

They all screamed at the same time.

Californika and Angela hugged each other and hysterically jumped up and down.

"Twins. Yes twins. I love twins. Wow twins!"

The women celebrated at the news.

The midwife handed the baby to Californika before attending to Karolina.

She cleaned the area between her legs with a cloth.

"Relax take your time and then push again." said the midwife holding Karolina's leg.

After another session the second twin baby was born. Karolina was very exhausted, but the thoughts of twins gave her enough energy to push.

When the second baby came out, there was so much joy the midwife had never witnessed before. Karolina cried holding both her kids.

Angela pushed the bedroom door open. Karolina was lying on the bed. Angela was holding one of the twins in her hands. Karolina raised her head and looked at her.

"Yes."

Angela breathed heavily and walked closer to Karolina.

"My beautiful baby. Come to your mummy."

"What's wrong Angie you look like you have seen a ghost. Sleepless nights?"

Angela breathed heavily.

"I don't understand why the baby cried all night. It's the second night in a row."

Karolina looked lost.

"The second night? Why didn't you wake me up?"

Angela sat on the bed next to Karolina.

"I didn't want to trouble you. Just thought I let you have a good sleep until your turn to babysit."

"You should have woken me up. Might have been something serious."

"I thought maybe just another rough night."

Karolina stopped looking at the baby and looked straight at Angela.

"And?"

Angela looked down.

"What is it? Tell me. What's wrong? Are they having a fever or what? Maybe call the doctor?"

"I thought a fever at first."

"So, what is it Angie?"

Karolina handed the baby to Angie and grabbed the phone.

"I don't think you will need a doctor?"

Karolina stopped and looked at Angela who in turn lifted the baby in the air and played with the baby.

"You are scaring me now."

Angela placed the baby on her lap upside down and lifted its top to reveal its side rib-cage. Karolina knelt and took a quick glance and instantly looked at Angela.

"What is that? I swear that was not there the last time I bathed the baby. When was it?"

She looked at Angela thinking.

She looked at the mark on the underarm rib-cage.

"A day ago, after the first night the baby had a sleepless night I noticed raised marks, but I just brushed that aside. I assumed the baby might have slept on something. You know?"

"Are you saying that this happened just last night? Is it why the baby cried all night?" asked Karolina touching the raised part on the baby's body.

"It looks like a ..." instantly Karolina looked at Angela.

"Tattoo," said the women at the same time.

Karolina quickly entered the twin's bedroom and grabbed the other twin and quickly checked him.

Angela entered the twin's bedroom and looked at Karolina.

"Both the same night but surprisingly him he did not cry at all."

The two women took turns to inspect all the babies. They glanced at each other.

"So, are you saying that the tattoos became pronounced just this morning?"

The women sat down.

"Do you believe in supernatural?"

"I would like to believe and think myself as a scientist and to answer you, no."

"So how would you explain this?"

Karolina looked at Angela. She got up and walked in the bedroom. She stopped, and her face fumed with rage.

"I think they are tampering with our kids."

"Who?"

"The doctors and or the hospital?"

"The babies had no markings the day we left the hospital? The marks only appeared recently, and we haven't been in contact with any doctor?"

Karolina sat down and covered her face.

"Bastards! Doctor's nowadays have become the devils and the vehicles of evil. Technological development has meant advanced tricks as well."

"Why you dislike doctors this much?" fumed Angela.

"Doctors should be the most trusted and should be people of good standing not these scams easily used by politicians."

"I am just saying be objective. How can a doctor tattoo an infant and why?"

"These doctors they are trying to create a dependency situation so that in the future it's easy to predict our movements. They torture our baby knowing that we are going to phone them to seek for help. Can't you see it?"

Angela got up and walked in the bedroom.

"What for. I don't get it?"

"I know you don't get it. I said these people are evil. No human being would do such a thing to one another. I swear I will kill all. They can't do that to my kids."

"Still it doesn't explain the tattoo. How did they do it?"

Karolina got up and walked to the babies and looked at them.

"Laser. Can do that if remotely controlled and operated using drone software."

"Are you saying that they planted IMDs in our kids?"

"They might have chipped our kids without our knowledge and consent say fired a chip just after birth when they took our kids."

"What for? I think you are just afraid to admit it that there is a power so powerful out there doing all this. Why don't you believe in God?"

"Don't be fooled. There is no such thing as supernatural. These evil doctors they trick and deceive people creating a dependency situation. I swear I will kill all. No one messes up with my kids."

Karolina sat down and breathed heavily.

"Sometimes I wish Nick was here."

Angela hugged Karolina and kissed her.

"I think we should call a priest. I don't think a doctor will be able to explain this."

A car parked outside a huge house. A priest got out and straightened his gown before proceeding in the yard before he knocked the door the door instantly opened. Angela and Karolina stood at the door with great expectations.

"We are glad you came straight away. Please come on in."

The priest entered the house holding his bible and a rosary. He stood in the lounge but was asked to follow Karolina into the kids' bedroom.

The babies lay on their bed flipping the legs into the air. Instantly they stopped and looked attentively at the priest before both bursting into cries. The two women looked at each other.

"There are too many evil spirits in this house?"

The two women held each other and looked at the priest. The priest took out his rosary he had worn round his neck and placed it in the hand.

The babies cried even louder.

"I command you in the name of God. Spirits leave now!"

The babies cried even louder.

The priest took the Torch Book and read a verse from the book.

The babies' cries become even louder.

"I need water."

"Tap water father?" asked Angela.

"Yes. I will pray for it."

The priest recited a prayer dosing the kids with water.

He looked at Karolina and made a sign on the kids.

Instantly as soon as the priest touched the kids, the babies instantly stopped crying. The two women looked at each other.

The priest recited a prayer before looking at the markings.

The priest looked at the twin's tattoos.

"What is that father?"

He looked at the tattoos again.

"Some kind of symbol or mark.?"

"Your kids are the chosen ones."

Karolina pinched Angela and threw a quick glance at her.

"Let's hear what he has to say first," whispered Angela.

The priest placed the kids' side by side and noted the two tattoos at the same time. He instantly looked surprised and looked at the two women.

"Have you heard about the Holy Torch?"

"No!"

"For it is written that identical twins will be born, and they will get the Torch restored to its clan and make us a people again."

The two women looked at each other. Karolina's face shone with much happiness.

"They are chosen? Chosen to do what?"

The priest inspected the tattoos again.

"Please sit down. It is a prophecy that the two Holy ones will be the vehicles in locating the Torch and they are the ones who will restore the Holy Torch."

"We have no clue as to what you are talking about."

"Generations after generations our people have failed to get back the stolen Torch."

"Stolen!" shouted the women at the same time.

"Yes, stolen Torch."

"I thought they said that the Torch was confiscated because the Leaders couldn't pay back the loan."

"No. The Torch was the symbol of peace and prosperity. It was the only way the Leaders could save money and invest. Long time ago there were no banks. The Leaders realized that they had to collect money for building a compound like a small city. They gathered all their resources in the form of gold and diamonds and all precious minerals. They asked the local smith to save all these. The local smith made this valuable Torch with the people's savings at that time in the form of gold, diamonds and minerals. The years that followed the Leaders borrowed secured loans using the Torch as collateral."

"More like a secured loan with the Torch as collateral?"

"Yes. You can say that. The Leader took the Torch and used it as a deposit with the landowners. It was like deposit money in the bank. He was guaranteed interest every month. There was nothing to lose as gold and diamonds prices increased. The value of the Torch increased significantly. The Leader realized that he can increase the value of the people at the same time enabling them to save. He told everyone that he had secured a loan to build the compound where the Torch would be housed and used the Torch as collateral. He asked everyone for money to pay back the loan every month. He collected this money every month. After the agreed time. The Leader got back the Torch and placed it in the newly built Torch Hall."

The two women listened to the priest attentively.

"In order not to lose the Torch the Leader asked the people to keep on paying the monthly payments which he further deposited. Over the years the value of the Torch increased as well as the deposits. The people were rich. The Leader wrote rules to make sure that they won't lose the Torch and to deter greediness."

"Does that explain the Torch Book?"

"That is correct."

"See over the years the Leaders and the people had the compound like their own city with a place of worship, houses and shopping malls. They flourished. They paid money for accommodation and facilities as well. They still paid savings in the form of Torch monthly fees."

"How come they ended up in debt and losing the Torch."

"They were the first to settle there. The land was theirs. The new owner even without correct title deeds advised them to move. The Leaders refused to move because the land was theirs in the first place."

"Is it why they killed the Leader?"

"Correct. To instill fear, they killed the leader and secretly threatened his son. Since they had huge savings and the Torch, his son and the other Leaders agreed to pay to buy back the land even if it was theirs in the first place."

"So how come they ended up losing the Torch."

"The 'land owner' later claimed that all their savings were his because all the monthly payments they paid for the Torch were for the tax collections on his land therefore collected on his behalf. He confiscated all the money and on top of that claimed that all the minerals including the gold were mined illegally from his land. Stolen to use his word. So, the Torch technically his."

The two women looked at each other.

"I don't see why my sons have anything to do with this?"

Karolina and Angela hugged each other.

"Over the years the Torch has been moved from one place to another so that no one knows exactly where it is. Over the years they have created replicas, so no one will know exactly where the Torch is. The former 'land owner' has been devious taking advantage of the people."

"What do you mean?"

"Still collecting the Torch's monthly payments and as well as taxes for the land."

"So, are you saying that they wrote the Torch Book just to keep the Torch with the people?"

"Yes. The former Leader was very clever. He tricked people believing that the Torch was Holy and therefore has to be a symbol of faith and religion."

"Was it not?" asked Angela.

"A way to bring the people together. A way to collect taxes indirectly. A way to establish common savings. Mind you there were no banks those days. A way to bring everyone together by placing it in the Torch Hall. A way to save the national resources and get secured loans to build houses and to collect rent on all houses."

"Just like today's system?"

"Yes. Same principle."

"I don't believe you. The Torch Book was written by God through man," quipped Angela.

"I give everyone all the facts. It's up to you to accept what to believe. If you believe that story good for you but if you are like me, you will see God's hand at work. God created man and guided man through the Holy Torch Book ways to handle life. The Torch Book's words must be fulfilled. We long to be a people again for without the Torch we have no freedoms, riches and rights to everything. The Torch belonged to us. Today I have witnessed the work of God. I have seen the two Holy ones who will restore the Torch. The marks on their bodies will guide them for they are the marks of the Holy God."

Karolina stood up and walked to the window.

"You are being fooled. Can't you see what they are doing."

"Karolina if you don't believe don't turn people against their religion," advised Angela.

"Let me talk. Hear my side of the story. These crooks they do this every year or after certain periods."

"Here we go again," whispered Angela.

"Can't you see it. They let you work hard and save your money. When you about to spend the money on your family and loved ones they create these situations."

"Why would they go to such lengths? What do they get?"

Karolina laughed.

"They are still collecting the Torch monthly fees, but this will mean more people paying more money to them. Every time there is a sign, my twins for that matter there is fear and people cooperate fearing for their lives. People pay more with the hope that the Torch will be found. They long for the Torch because they associate the Torch with uprisings for freedom.

The Torch reminds them of the people who died trying to secure land for their people. The Torch with all the gold and diamonds is a symbol of wealth. People easily donate and offer them loans because they have assets they can use as collateral. They all know this, and they take advantage of this as well."

"These people and we ourselves strongly believe in the Torch Book and the prophecy and we can use the same arguments that first and foremost it's religion that plays a big role. We fight because we believe in the Torch and the book. We can never be a people without the Torch, our Torch. Until we secured it back, we shall pay whatever we can afford to get the Torch back. Simply because it is ours and have the right to possess and own it."

"The tattoos on my twins are they symbols of the Torch?"

"Yes. I also think they are part of a map to where they will find the Torch."

Karolina laughed.

"I am not trying to be funny, but you are telling me that God imprinted these tattoos on my twin's ribs?"

"Yes. It is a prophecy and one that shall come true."

"Please! It's these evil doctors. Somehow they have fired a chip into our kids and are using it with remote control and laser technology to torture my twins."

"I have never heard of such a thing."

"Angela you should know better than this."

"What do you mean Karolina?"

"All the crying was cries of pain as these evils remotely attacked and tortured our twins. Surely I am going to kill these evils."

Karolina started sobbing.

"It's so evil and inhumane. I have seen people being tried in Hague for lesser crimes."

The priest sat down for a while.

"Madam. Let me explain your kids' roles in all this?"

"Nick!"

A limousine parked outside a huge mansion. The driver got out and opened the door. A man smartly dressed up got out and walked inside the yard of the mansion. A huge dog came out wriggling its tail hysterically. The man knelt and rubbed the dog. The man continued walking until he reached the door to the mansion. A quick knock and the door opened. The house maiden opened the door.

"Can I get you any refreshments?"

"No thanks I am okay."

"Where is he?"

"Been in the study room since morning."

Alexander was one of the businessmen who was selected by the Leaders to represent them. It was a welcome and very appreciated gesture considering that the Leaders was a group of very rich yet old businessmen. Alexander was young in his mid-forties. The Leaders had chosen him to represent them because of his charms and negotiating skills. He emitted confidence and riches even though his business was facing difficulties above all his father had been a member of the leaders the time he died. Alexander straightened his suit and adjusted the position of his tie before knocking the study room door.

"Come on in. Take a seat."

Alexander smiled genuinely before walking to the center of the study room.

"We can finish later," said Kai talking to the nude painting model.

"What can I do for you Alex,"

"Business as usual."

"Business?"

"What I don't understand is that why do I still have to pay these people surely when my father died that should have been it."

Kai just looked at him and sighed.

"I am not making any money even the little I am making they come for it all the time."

"Did they pay you a visit again?"

"The worst part of all this is that I don't even know how he ended up in this mess."

Kai walked and sat in his comfy seat.

"I wish I can tell you, but we made an oath."

"So, what are you saying? I represent you and you keep secrets away from me?"

Alexander sighed with disbelief.

"Like I said all these years it's for your own good."

"Kai how can that be for my own good when I am losing money?"

Kai stood up and walked toward the window and looked outside. He then walked to the painting he had painted.

"Hmm what do you think?"

Alexander sighed and then walked toward the painting. He just looked at the painting before looking at Kai.

"Surely I think there must be a way. I am not a kid anymore. We have to end this somehow."

Kai smiled and moved very closer to the painting.

"Not quite what I wanted."

He looked at Alexander and walked toward him before touching his shoulder.

"You reminded me of myself when I was your age. Look at me now. What do you think I can do?

Priorities have changed. If I had a son surely, he is the one who would be doing all this. They are clever you know they wait until…."

"How is Andrea?"

"Alright?"

Kai smiled before sitting.

"So, what happened to you? How did you lose hope?"

"Let's just say I became a family man."

"So, this can never be resolved or what?"

"Ever wondered why we choose you to be a member of the Leaders? For generations the Leaders comprised the 'Leaders' only. I looked for the past generations and realized that when the time to collect we all will be very old to bother about all this. Our fathers failed and their fathers before that. You are our hope. Your father's death has become somehow a blessing in that we included you in the Leaders.

"All the money should have been paid by now."

Kai stood up and walked toward the painting.

"It all started when your father died."

He stopped and looked at Alexander.

"Your father was the wisest and the stronger one of us. We choose him to represent us. What did we know those days?"

Kai took a paint brush and corrected an area on the painting.

"Although it was a collective decision everything went through your father."

He paused for a while.

"When he died, it was a shock to us."

Alexander walked toward the window.

"No one ever expected that."

Kai walked to his chair and sat down.

"After he died, we realized that we had made a mistake. I personally approached them and offered everything we owed them, so we get it back."

There was silence for a while.

"Yes, go on I am listening," said Alexander.

"They refused."

"What?"

"They claimed that they had met again with your father shortly before his death."

"Yes."

"They said that he had come back for more money without us and since he was the representative, they believed him and increased the loan."

Alexander's face creased with rage.

"I felt the same too."

"That can't be right. Where did he put the money? My father would never do that."

"Ever since they kept asking for a higher settling value."

"What do we do now?"

The two men looked at each other.

"Hard to say. They have passed laws to weaken and dismantle the Leaders. They say that belongs to them now that the Leaders have disregarded the agreement."

"What agreement? It was a robbery in the first place. They are all accessories to a murder, bloody thieves. They killed my father."

"Even their leader is trying to make it look right when it was a bloody murder in the first place. The whole institution is corrupt the whole government is evil. How can you justify a murder and a daylight robbery in the first place?"

"Maybe let someone else translate maybe if that is happening to them they might understand."

"Alex that's not the way to go around it."

Alex fumed with rage.

"It's an insult. My father died for nothing and now publicly they are trying to make it look right. If that happened to them do you think they will react the same way?"

"Only you can solve this. We have all our hopes in you. Look, we are running out of time. For years we have done the same thing and still failed. We were hoping that you might be our answer. We must fulfill the prophecy. We have longed to be a people again."

"What can I do?"

"A wise man, your father to be specific once told me that your strength can be your weakness too."

"I am not following."

"I have never thought about it, what he really meant but it's clear to me now."

Kai touched Alexander's shoulder.

"If they can do this to your father and to us, they can also do this to others."

"You have to go out there and find the others."

In another city three luxurious cars parked outside a mansion in the suburb. The men hurriedly entered the mansion. Inside the mansion lifts took them down to the bunker underneath. Inside was well decorated with huge screens on the walls. There were comfy seats surrounding the middle sofa. Inside was dim with fading lighting that you could see fading shadows. Inside was a man well dressed up wearing cross-belts. He looked unamused and rarely smiled. The other men sat down in the seats as if they had their names written on them. It seemed they had gathered here many times before that it was on their finger tips that they simply know where to be and what to do. The man in the center was Eric the chairman of the bank. The other men were Kevin the managing director. Kyle, the CEO and Brody the regional director of the bank.

"Gentlemen this is an unusual meeting and thanks for coming at such a short notice."

Eric passed around some documents. The other men took their copies and looked at them for a while.

"We are all obligated to safeguard the bank's money. We have a duty to intervene when things are not going as planned. Looking at the figures in front of you, you can see that we have lost a huge amount in the tune of $ billions to robberies and other losses."

The man nodded looking at each other.

"I have decided to set up our own secret investigating team. I know you are going to say that we follow protocol and leave everything with the local authorities. But."

"Protocol true. We don't want any duplication, better use of the shareholder's money. Remember?"

intervened Kevin.

"We are going to lose this money anywhere. I suggest we become proactive."

The men looked at each other first and then at Eric.

Giovanni opened the car door leaving it open and

staggered outside. He returned and closed the door before heading to the house. A quick knock at the door and a half-naked woman opened the door.

"You are drunk again?"

The woman looked upset and walked in to the lounge.

"Giovanni! Are you hearing me? How can you do this to me? If you don't want to start a family with me why can't you just say so?"

"I am sorry babes."

"That's not good enough. We talked about this."

"We can still do it."

"I want you sober. I want healthy kids."

"So, what did you find out?"

The woman walked in the bedroom and brought a huge gown and covered her body.

"You won't believe it."

Giovanni appeared sober as he sat up straight to hear what the woman had to say.

"On all occasions it was more of a collection than a bank robbery."

"What do you mean?"

"No struggle at all."

"So, what are we looking at here?"

"The only similar situation I have heard is in protection situations?"

"What do you mean? Do you mean as in mafia circles?"

"Exactly!"

"Holy Sugar!"

"Tell me about it."

"OK. Let's say your presumption is correct who will be behind all this? Why would the banks pay protection money?"

Over the following weeks Giovanni and Sienna tried to solve and identify the bank robbers with no luck. One-night Giovanni came home early and very sober. He had a wine bottle and some roses. He entered the lounge and called for Sienna. He proceeded to the bedroom leaving the roses on the bed.

"Darling, where are you?" shouted Giovanni.

Quickly he left the bedroom and headed downstairs to the study room in the basement.

"What's wrong?" said Giovanni looking at Sienna.

Sienna was wearing track bottoms and a big jumper. This was the first time he had returned home to find his sexy girlfriend not in lingerie waiting for him.

"I am sober and ready for you. I am all yours."

"What? A taste of your own medicine. How many times have I waited for you while you come home drunk? I am fed up. Come I want to show you something," said Sienna pulling Giovanni's hand.

Giovanni wore a sad face.

"It better be good."

Sienna's face shined as she talked to Giovanni.

"I checked all the bank robberies and correlated this information to the information of all hotel occupants at the time of the robbery. Check out what I came up with."

Giovanni unfastened his bow tie and looked at the computer screen. He looked shocked and looked at Sienna.

"Who is Cynthia Banks?"

The couple glanced at each other.

Cynthia after talking to Bradley on the phone walked very fast looking back frequent. A car screeched its tires around the corner. Cynthia's instincts kicked in that she sprinted very fast escaping between pedestrians.

The shop windows were smashed by bullets and the noise made Cynthia duck for cover. Screams made by the people left the others taking cover as well. The car passed at speed before coming to a sudden stop in the middle of the road ahead. Cynthia got up and ran for her life. Instantly the car reversed before suddenly swerving making a U-turn in the road. Cynthia entered the mall. She looked behind to see if someone was coming. She bumped into a woman carrying bags sending her parcels all over the floor. The woman screamed before kneeling to pick up her parcels. Cynthia entered the elevator nervously and pressed the buttons hysterically. The doors were about to close when fingers held the door preventing it closing. Cynthia's heart beat instantly became elevated. She froze with fear. A man suddenly entered the lift.

"Close. Close. Fast!" shouted Cynthia peeping in the corridor.

"Are you sure you are okay?"

Cynthia stood in the corner of the elevator shaking nervously. She looked at the elevator indicator. The elevator bell rung, and the man instantly looked at Cynthia.

"Sure, you are okay?"

Cynthia peeped behind the man and as soon as he had left she frantically pressed the buttons. She left the elevator as soon as the door opened. She headed to the parking area. She opened the car door and jumped in. She looked in the direction she came. She started the car then suddenly the elevator door opened. A man stood there for a split second before he sprinted toward the car as the engine noise directed him where to go. He instantly stopped as the car reversed and pulled his gun and aimed at the car. The first bullet missed. Cynthia screamed while looking back as the car reversed. She quickly stopped the car, changed the gears quickly and looked ahead raving the car. A second bullet smashed the side mirror. She knew another shot she could not be that lucky. She stepped on the gas pedal and drove toward the man. The man fired shots before spinning away from the car's path. Cynthia's car left the car park at speed and disappeared. The man ran out of the car park and stopped outside before from the other side an SUV approached. The man jumped inside before the SUV made the chase.

Far away Bradley was busy checking the information being captured by the huge industrial-like computers when the ringing of his cellphone startled him. He looked at the cellphone screen and noticed that it was Cynthia calling. Quickly he grabbed his stuff and left the underground room. He entered the elevator and when the doors were about to close he saw two men quickly entering the room he was in. His heart beat shot up. Quickly he pressed the elevator buttons. He reached the ground level and flashed his ID to the first security man he met. He walked very fast toward the exit. In the long corridor he reached the middle when two men suddenly appeared behind him. He looked at them and took the corner very fast before sprinting for his life. The two men followed very fast pulling guns as they followed. He quickly pressed the exit buttons, and the doors opened instantly. Another man had just entered the building.

"Stop him!"

Bradley quickly flashed his ID before escaping the building. He ran as fast as he can toward his car. The man fired shots. He didn't stop he carried on until he reached his car. He threw his laptop bag on the passenger seats and drove away quickly. The two fired several shots shattering the back-window screen.

CHAPTER EIGHT

Detective Kristy was sleeping when her cellphone rang. Instantly she picked up the cellphone.

"OK I will be there."

Detective Kristy walked in the building in the city center. Detective Braden came from the other side to meet her.

"I think we got our robbers."

"If you say so." replied Detective Kristy.

"What?" asked Detective Braden stopping and flipping the file before looking at the other Detective.

"You don't believe me?"

In the lab Evan a tall slim lab technician handed the

report to Detective Braden.

"Somehow we have managed to identify these two as our suspects."

Detective Kristy took the file and looked at the profile.

"Witness statements referred to more than two people. These two don't fit the profile of a group of people four to five middle-aged men."

"They have been in the hotels in the robbed cities at the time the banks were robbed. Good enough for me."

"No witnesses ever mentioned a woman being part of the gang."

"How can they tell when they were all wearing masks?"

"Okay what do we know about the woman?"

"Mid-twenties. School dropout. High spending patterns. Source of income undisclosed. Checked in the hotels of robbed cities at the same time the robberies happened."

Detective Kristy walked to the other side.

"Maybe they were set up."

"What would be the motive?"

"I am just saying if they were to rob the bank they would have checked in with false names."

"What are the chances of banks robbed in all cities at the same time when they had checked in in the cities' hotels?"

"Boyfriend?"

"Yes. But for some reasons he only checked in the first robbery and I think after that he used a different name."

"OK the boyfriend might be involved or is linked. What more do we know about him?"

Cynthia walked into the bathroom and looked at herself in the big mirrors. She breathed heavily. Bradley entered the bathroom and hugged her from behind. He kissed her all over.

"We should go far away from here. I have a gut feeling that they might start looking for us."

"Don't worry we are safe here."

Detective Kristy got in her car and sat for a while. She took out her cellphone and dialed a number.

Detective Braden answered the phone.

"Do you want to go around for a while? I am fed up of sitting and waiting?"

"Kind of in the middle of something I will pass."

The car sped away heading toward the suburbs.

Bradley entered the bedroom. Cynthia was lying on the bed facing down.

"Can you give me a massage before I go to sleep?"

Bradley jumped on top of her and sat on her.

"I think we have to go to Latvia. It starts to make sense now. Some months ago, I received a telephone call from the bank there."

"What did they say?"

"I think I have another account opened for me when I first started this job. I had a canceled assignment there."

"So, what's stopping us?"

"I need some documents from our house."

"No. We can't go there."

"I know but I can."

"No. Bradley. You can't leave me here alone."

"So, come with me then."

"Can we do this tomorrow? I have to sleep now."

"Don't worry I won't be long I will be back before you know it. You will be safe here."

Cynthia quickly got up and wore her clothes and sat on the bed.

"You know it's dangerous. Someone might be there expecting us to return."

"I will be careful. I love you."

"Maybe we should go back together."

"Don't worry I will be back soon."

Bradley kissed Cynthia and left the bedroom.

"Make sure that all the doors are locked okay?"

Cynthia heard the car speeding away and waited for Bradley to return.

Bradley's car entered the street to his house, and he switched off the headlights. He parked away from the house and waited. After a while a car driven by a woman passed his parked car. He had already ducked the moment it entered the street. He raised his head to see who was driving. As the car approached his house it slowed down, and the woman looked at the house attentively before the car disappeared. Bradley's heart beat shot up. He thought for a while before dismissing his fears. He waited again for a while before finding courage. He left his car and walked toward his house. No one was home as far as he knew. He opened the front door and entered the house stealthily. He didn't waste any time he collected the documents he needed and left the house. He checked if it was clear before going back to his car. He stood outside his car and opened the door.

"Freeze don't move, or I will shoot."

Bradley felt a strange feeling of fear that he froze for a split second.

"I am unarmed. I have documents in my hands. Don't shot!"

Turn around nice and slowly.

"Who are you? What do you want?"

"Let's just say your worst enemy. They want you dead or alive."

Bradley quickly turned and looked at the woman holding a gun before throwing the documents at her and running for his life.

The woman fired a shot in the air.

"Stop or I will shoot!"

That fell on deaf ears as Bradley had already run away. The woman chased after him, but he had already gone.

"Damn it!"

Instantly her cellphone rang.

She looked at the cellphone and noticed that it was her boss ringing.

"I nearly got the suspect!" shouted Detective Kristy breathing heavily.

"They are not ready. Leave them. That's an order."

"But Sir."

The call abruptly ended.

She walked back and picked up the documents he had thrown in her face. She walked to her car and sat in before ringing Detective Braden.

Giovanni and Sienna entered the bedroom kissing

and hugging each other before throwing themselves onto the bed.

"Come on top," suggested Sienna.

"You know what? Give me back."

Giovanni started kissing Sienna's back passionately while his hands were caressing her thighs. Instantly a beep sound went off.

They both stopped and looked at each other.

Giovanni got up and took out his pager.

"They got the bank robbers."

Sienna got up and wore her clothes very fast before the pair sat in front of the television in the lounge.

The anchorwoman was on the television.

"A man and woman were shot dead by the police today. They are believed to be the ones who have terrorized the banks in the past months. No one can comment regarding this, but the mood is that of celebrating. Stacy reporting."

The couple looked at each other.

"Makes no sense."

"Why?"

"The police shot them?"

"That's what the woman said."

"Take your jacket let's go."

The pair left the house and into the car before driving off. Giovanni stepped on the gas pedal and drove like a rally driver. A lot of questions were going through in his mind.

"There are the last people I expected to kill these suspects."

"What are we missing here?"

"I think they know a lot."

Giovanni after a telephone call headed to the lab research facility in the city.

Detective Bradley came out and as he was walking to his car Giovanni and Sienna approached him.

"Excuse me Detective we are reporters and have a few questions to ask you."

"Sorry I can't help you on that."

"We all know that these two don't fit the profiles of the bank robbers."

"Like I said no comment."

"Honestly you are the last ones we suspected to have killed these two."

The detective stopped and looked at Giovanni.

"What are you implying?"

I am saying that you know more than you are admitting to.

"Choose your words very carefully."

"What are you hiding Detective?" asked Giovanni.

"Nothing. We believe they robbed those banks. They were in all the cities at the time the banks were robbed that's good enough for me."

"How can they fit the profile of a group of middle-aged men?"

"Either way they are involved."

"Maybe someone is setting them up Detective?"

The detective stopped and looked at Giovanni.

"I don't like the sound of it."

"Maybe they decided to get rid of the evidence?"

"Watch it! No more comments."

"And you are helping them clean their mess. Is that so?"

Giovanni followed the detective still asking more questions, but the detective walked fast to his car before driving off.

That evening the couple sat and looked at each other speechless.

"We should have located them first. We might have got the answers we need."

"We did our best."

"I think there is more they are covering up. Something bigger than just the bank robberies."

Giovanni got up quickly and went to the study room.

For the next weeks he searched repeatedly for clues but with no luck. Sienna weeks later arrived home with a copy of the suspected bank robber's autopsy report. Giovanni set up search parameters. Sienna slumped down next to Giovanni and started smiling.

"Today let's just spend the whole day making-up. In the last months all we did was worry about this project. There is nothing we can do. We might never know who was behind the bank robberies."

The couple all night made love until they all fell asleep. A beep sound went off, but they were both too fast asleep to take notice. Sienna woke up to go to the bathroom. On her way back, the flashing light of the pager caught her attention. She went to the study room and looked at the printed report on the printer. She sat down and started searching further looking at the report.

"Oh my God! Giovanni come and see this."

Giovanni woke up disoriented and staggered to the study room.

"Look at this," she showed Giovanni the report.

He looked at the report and then at Sienna.

"What is it?"

"Sit down and look at all the reports what do you notice?"

"I am lost. What am I supposed to see?"

asked Giovanni.

"We all know that they set up these two, so I asked myself why kill these? Obvious to cover up something. So, whatever they are covering will have similarities or say patterns to these two presumed robbers. So, I looked at death records too. I checked people who died at the same time as these two. Look at the report."

Giovanni looked for a while without saying anything.

He ran another report, and the couple looked at each other as the computer processed the results.

There were a hundred people who died exactly at the same time as Bradley and a hundred who died at the same time as Cynthia in all the cities the robberies took place.

Giovanni looked at Sienna and went a further step researching.

"They all had insurance policies with the two major insurance companies."

"Have you ever heard about digital-soul collectors?"

"No. What are they?"

"These are the few unfortunate people who are chosen because they are perceived as weak and are abused by the doctors before they are assigned a digital-gun."

"Digital-gun? What's that?"

"Digital-killers. The doctors collect pain and stress feelings and then convert these to the digital format. They look at the people who have insurance policies. People who are rich, etc. They locate these and link them to these two digital-soldiers. They pay for the digital-soldiers activities sending them everywhere. They live luxurious lives in hotels weekend after the other traveling around the country even abroad."

"Do they know that they are digital-soldiers?"

"No, they have no idea. They are told that they are collecting vital information and at times they do collect information."

"What are you saying?"

"Most of the times they are distributing the digitally converted pain and misery everywhere searching for souls to collect."

"You mean weakening and killing?"

"They are regarded as catalysts or assassins."

"But still that does not explain why they would all die at the same time miles apart."

Giovanni stopped and looked at Sienna.

"Or they are just used to link themselves to these people before whoever is behind this kill everyone at the same time. Then collects the insurance money?"

"Still insurance money goes to the relatives. They all can't have no relatives."

Giovanni paced for a while up and down.

"Unless…"

"Yes, I am listening."

"Unless the insurance policies were taken without their knowledge."

Giovanni searched for insurance records.

"What is Future-digital-insurance? Let's go let's pay them a visit."

Detective Kristy entered the office she shared with Detective Braden.

"Good morning Detective."

"Morning so early today?"

"Couldn't sleep last night."

There was a moment of silence.

"Still having nightmares?"

"Not really just this case."

"This case?"

"I think they were set up. Even still, you didn't have to kill them."

Detective Bradley got up before putting on a creased face. He walked toward the window.

"I had no option. It could have been me. Don't make me feel guilty. It happened in a split second. He had a gun."

"I still don't believe you."

"Damn it! Detective. How many times do I have to tell you? You were in that situation before."

"He nearly pissed his pants with fear."

"He had a gun!" shouted Detective Braden.

"He threw his documents at me and ran away."

"I don't know maybe he got smarter this time. Whose side are you on anywhere?"

"I am just saying not a typical bank robber. Just a stupid young man."

"Listen we have $millions stolen everywhere, and the boss was breathing down my neck for answers. It happens. Okay."

Detective Kristy got up and walked to the window.

She looked outside for a while.

"I have been to the lab. I have seen the report."

She threw piercing eyes at Detective Braden.

Detective Braden sat down.

"Okay Detective tell me again."

"Okay."

He paused and breathed hard.

"He had a gun. Instincts kicked in."

There was a moment of silence.

"Okay Detective I will tell you what happened even

though I was not there."

Detective Braden smiled sarcastically and gave the floor to Detective Kristy.

"Your pager went off. You got a tip off. You pretended that you were following your instincts. Surprised, you came face-to-face with the couple, then you cornered them. You point a gun at them. Surprised and afraid too to see you they panicked. They are unarmed. You tried to call for back-up but somehow your cellphone rang. You answered it and the boss gave you an order."

"What order?"

"To shoot them."

"He had a gun!"

"You first objected preferring to take them to the station, but the boss insisted that you shoot them, and you have nothing to worry about."

There was silence in the room.

"Is that what happened Detective?"

The detective remained silent.

"Did you receive a phone call too?"

Detective Kristy nodded.

"Damn it! I had no choice."

Detective Kristy looked outside the window.

"Who is behind all this?"

"Complicated. Let's just say at least something good is going to come out of all this."

"Something good? Detective. I took an oath to serve and to protect and this is definitely not it."

Detective Braden smiled.

"They were in every city that was robbed."

"So?"

"They are part of the first versions of the digital-soldiers, the information gatherers to be precise?"

"Meaning?"

"Meaning they recorded and collected information of what happened, and we can only have access to this classified information if they are implicated and dead otherwise data protection and human rights laws won't allow us."

Detective Braden smiled.

"Are you saying that they are framing up all these people so as to use the information to implicate and convince the public?"

"It's called effective harvesting. We can now get our real bank robbers."

Detective Kristy sat down and covered her face.

"What did I get myself into?"

CHAPTER NINE

An expensive car parked in the hotel car park. Delta a tall and above average handsome man with pronounced short hair, a clean shave and a dimple on his chin smiled at the car park attendant. The woman smiled back taking Delta's luggage inside the hotel. Delta walked with a style like a male-model. The hotel lobby was busy with people inside sat on the comfy seats. At the desk was a very beautiful blond lady. He looked at her and smiled. He leaned against the desk and looked in the lobby for a while before turning back at the receptionist.

"Bellissimo! Beautiful!"

"Good atmosphere to relax and wind down."

"Exactly what I need, madam."

After checking in Delta entered his luxurious hotel

room. The room was very huge with a double bed in the middle and a huge mirror on the ceiling above the bed. He smiled and pressed the mattress down.

"Lovely. Perfect."

He walked to the table and placed his bag and gently opened one of the bags. He took out his laptop and checked something. Instantly his face started shaking with rage. His` face creased with anger. His voice became raucous in tone.

"Why are they taking too long? Where is my money?"

He quickly sat on the bed. He opened the bag and took out a gun. He opened a small box which he had taken out from his bag. Inside was a silk cloth. He started polishing his gun. Blowing air and leaving steam on it.

He stood up and walked to the bathroom. He looked in the mirror. He smiled for a split second before his face started showing rage patterns like an animal about to attack. He started shaking and instantly he pulled his gun and aimed in the mirror. Instantly he calmed down. He looked in the mirror at proximity before wiping sweat pores tricking down his face.

He took a shower and left the hotel.

A limousine cruised picking up speed as it left the city center. The driver looked everywhere and saw a motorbike approaching When he looked again in the rear-view mirror the bike had disappeared.

Adam the CEO of Future-Digital-Insurance was in the limousine in the back seat. A bullet sound rocketed in the air and smashed the side window of the limousine.

"We are under attack. Drive!" shouted Adam taking cover.

The driver looked and saw a motorbike approaching from one side. The driver swerved the car instantly. Delta lifted the front wheel of the motorbike and as he passed the limousine's back seat, he pulled a gun and blasted the window open. Adam took cover. The driver swerved trying to hit the motorbike sideways but lost control sending the limousine skidding. He turned the steering wheel in the opposite direction until he straightened the limousine. Delta pulled back before increasing speed again. He lifted the gun and aimed but the limousine swerved. He placed the gun on his waist belt and held the motor bike with both wheels. On full speed he planned to overtake the limousine. He switched to full throttle and sped past the limousine only to turn around in the road ahead. He quickly pulled the gun and aimed at the driver. The driver's heart beat jumped up when he saw the gun pointed at him. He ducked quickly but held the steering wheel firm. The bullet shattered the window screen. He lifted his head but lost control of the limousine that it went off the road. Delta quickly started the motorbike and followed the limousine with one hand he held the gun tight aimed at the driver's door. He fired three shots before the driver had a chance to escape. He walked to the back of the limousine. Adam was between the back seats.

"Come out now. Easy, nice and slowly."

Instantly a bullet sound rocketed the skies.

Adam screamed in agony.

"Son of a beast! You shot me!"

"What?"

Delta quickly removed the helmet and stared at Adam.

Adam's face relaxed when he saw Delta's handsome face.

"Who are you? What do you want?"

"Don't be fooled. Looks can be deceiving. I am here to kill you."

"Why?"

Delta retrieved a picture from his jacket.

He looked at it and looked at Adam.

His face started shaking like an animal about to attack. The next time Adam looked at him. He saw evil in Delta's eyes. His handsome face had creased with rage. He opened his jacket pocket and retrieved a device that he screwed onto the barrel of the gun.

"I didn't do anything wrong to you."

"I know." he replied.

"But..."

"I don't want to know you, or your grievances or anything. Okay."

Once Delta had finished, he checked the camera he had screwed onto the barrel of the gun and aimed at Adam.

He fired two shots. Adam fell instantly. Delta's face relaxed. He walked to where Adam lay. He knelt next to him and searched his pockets. He retrieved his ID before jumping on his bike.

Detective Braden and Detective Kristy had just left the coroner's office when they stopped outside on the car park.

"I am confused now. Is there someone out there?"

Detective Braden's face showed signs of stress and anguish.

"You are not good at hiding your feelings, right?"

"I am not scared at all."

"So why do you act like you have seen a ghost?"

"Just trying to piece everything together."

"No doubt. Mark of an assassin. Shot at close range."

"Do we have any suspects?"

"I have one or two in mind. Come let's go."

Detective Braden drove for a while before starting a conversation.

"The whole system is fucked up you know."

He looked at Detective Kristy, but she did not look back.

"That's the norm."

"I guess that's the job."

"Would you have pulled the trigger?"

There was silence.

"You think I am a rotten cop. Right?"

"I didn't say that."

Detective Kristy didn't look at him.

"I know but it's written all over your face. Sometimes you don't have to say it, but I know."

"Are you judging me now?"

"I know you Detective in and out."

"What is that supposed to mean?"

There was silence.

"You can't even look at me nowadays. But I remember it clearly you nearly pissed your pants when he threw papers in your face."

Detective Kristy looked at him.

"I was in the same position. Either him or me?"

Detective Kristy looked upset.

"I can't stand it when you lie to me. How can I trust you? We are partners and you bloody lie to me? He had no gun."

Detective Braden harsh brakes sending the car skidding before it came to a halt.

"What are you doing?"

The driver's door instantly swung open. Detective Braden jumped out of the car and walked to the other side and opened the door.

"Come out! You are the saint one."

Detective Kristy remained in the car.

"Don't be stupid Detective let's go."

"No, we can't go like this. You are supposed to watch my back. How can we be partners when you can't even look at me in the face?"

"I don't know what you are talking about."

"Come out. Look at me face-to-face. I want to believe that when we arrive there, I can trust you and count on you."

Detective Braden pulled Detective Kristy out of the car.

"Take out your gun!"

"What?"

"You heard me. Take out your gun."

Detective Kristy was about to go back in the car when Detective Braden pulled out his gun and aimed at her.

"I said take out your gun."

Detective Kristy pulled her gun and aimed back.

"I told you he had a gun."

"Nonsense! We both know he had no gun. Stop upsetting me okay."

"Are you saying that I planted the gun?"

"What difference does it make if not you, then they did it for you?"

"If you are so sure maybe I will get rid of you too." replied Detective Braden putting on a devil's face.

Instantly Detective Kristy cocked up her gun. She firmly aimed at Detective Braden.

"Try and see!"

Detective Braden put his gun down.

"Shoot! Come on. Shoot!"

She looked at him still aiming the gun. She lowered the gun down and entered the car.

Detective Braden entered the car and drove without saying anything.

Sienna and Giovanni were cuddling after having sex.

"You are not afraid?"

"Why should I be?"

"I am just saying what if they tried to clean us too?" Giovanni sighed.

"I never thought it that way."

He looked at Sienna. He kissed her first.

"Maybe we should go on vacation for some time."

"Yes, once this is over..."

"What? We can't wait. I have a bad feeling about all this."

"I love you. Maybe you are right. We go any day, tomorrow, end of this week, I mean whenever you are ready."

"Okay darling."

Sienna jumped on top of Giovanni. She kissed him passionately.

"Fear makes me want you all the time."

"Nothing to be afraid of."

The couple made passionate love as much as they can before they all slumped onto the bed.

"I just want us to be like this forever."

"What if it's people with more power than we thought?"

Giovanni sighed without a word. For the first time he realized that danger was real. He hugged Sienna and imagined themselves living somewhere far away with their baby as they have always wished for.

"After this job we will have enough even for a house."

Sienna lifted her head and looked at Giovanni.

"Darling. Now you are acting like a grown up. That's what I wanted to hear from you. This baby thing was doing my head-in. I can relax now. I felt the pressure weighing me down. I love you Gio."

"I love you too, Sienna."

"Come."

Giovanni slowly weighed himself down on her. He could feel her warm body against his. He looked at her for a while. For the first time he felt like they had been married for years. She was the most beautiful lady he had laid eyes on. He felt her grip tightening more and more. He leaned down and kissed her passionately.

A car with the two detectives turned into a dark quiet street in one of the suburbs. The detective switched off the lights and drove silently and gently until the car came to a halt on the side of the road. The two detectives signaled before entering the property. Detective Braden signaled indicating that he will go via the back. Detective Kristy froze for a while. Detective Braden lowered his gun before going via the back door. Detective Kristy's heart beat elevated significantly. She approached the door and waited. She closed her eyes briefly and kicked the door. Quickly she entered the house. Instantly checked the kitchen, the lounge, the spare room before heading upstairs. Detective Braden entered via the backdoor waving his gun everywhere. He ran upstairs after hearing the commotion there.

"Don't move or I will shoot!" shouted Detective Kristy.

Sienna screamed covering herself. Giovanni had got up and worn his briefs.

"Don't point that thing at me?" shouted Giovanni.

"What do you want? You have no right to be in here?"

"I said don't move or I will shoot."

Detective Braden entered the bedroom pointing his gun.

"It's you, Detective?" Giovanni looked at the Detective.

"What is this all about?" asked Giovanni.

Sienna started crying hugging Giovanni. Giovanni hugged her back. The two detectives looked at each other.

Detective Kristy aimed firmly at Giovanni.

"What are you doing?" shouted Giovanni. Sienna screamed even louder. Detective Kristy looked at Detective Braden and shouted with a raised voice.

"He has a gun! He has a gun!" shouted Detective Kristy.

"Put your gun down now! I said put your gun down

now or I will shoot!"

The couple confused looked at each other and then at Detective Braden who in turn looked at them and lowered his gun while raising the other hand slowly before dropping the gun down.

Detective Kristy's shouting soon after that startled the couple especially Giovanni who switched instantly from looking at Detective Braden to looking at her.

"Put your gun down now! I said put your gun down now!"

Her pitch had risen so high that Giovanni just looked at her startled, confused and scared before two bullets lodged in his head. He slumped like a lifeless log. A scream instantly rocketed into the skies. The neighbors heard two more shots. The couple lay side by side dead in a pool of blood.

Detective Kristy walked outside the house and started puffing her electrical cigarette. Detective Braden looked at the couple and sighed. He looked at his gun on the floor and walked out of the house. He stood next to Detective Kristy.

"What were you thinking taking all that time? He could have shot you Detective?"

Detective Kristy looked at him and their eyes locked starring at each other for a very long time. Siren sounds could be heard from afar gradually becoming audible until the siren sounds filled the otherwise silent night.

A car stopped outside the buildings in the city center. Delta wearing sunglasses got out of the car and walked with style. He stopped half way and removed his glasses elegantly he blew warm breath on them before cleaning them with a white handkerchief. He was wearing a tight see through silk shirt that showed his well pumped body. He had a golden watch and a slim gold chain on his wrist. He had expensive black trousers and shinning Italian pointed shoes. He looked around and saw a beautiful lady walking on the other side of the road. The lady smiled sexily at the attention. He looked at his watch and touched his mouth in a posing way. She giggled even further. He pushed his hair backward and crossed the road to the other side. Half way through with his eyes fixed on the lady, a car came from nowhere and screeched its tires before stopping just a few feet away from him.

Delta froze for a while. He looked at the car and then at the woman driver. He looked at himself and straightened the pleats of his trousers.

"What the fuck are you doing? I could have killed you." shouted the female driver.

The woman from the other side of the road came running.

"Hey are you okay?"

She looked at him all over before looking at his face. She noticed that he was kind of shaking with his face shaking with rage. She touched his shoulder.

"He might be in shock." she suggested.

"Me in shock? No," replied Delta instantly removing his sunglasses and looking at the ladies. It amazed the women to see probably the most handsome man they have seen so far in their lifetime. A clean shave, shinning glittering eyes, a chin-dimple and a perfect smile.

"I am not in shock at all. I am just amazed to see such beauty in front of me. Bellissimo!" he kissed his fingertips and threw the kiss in the air.

"What?" asked the woman driver.

She touched her hair and looked at the other woman.

"I think he is still in shock I can take him to the hospital you can come too. Is he your boyfriend?"

"My boyfriend?" she whispered looking at him.

He raised his hand and hugged her before walking away from the road.

"I am in a hurry. If I can get your number, I promise I will phone you maybe take you to the lakeside."

"Yeah sure. Where are you going?"

"I cannot tell you, but I promise if we meet again I will tell you."

He smiled at her. She looked at him with longing even though they had just met. She felt goosebumps and weak inside. Delta walked with a style like a model and disappeared among the crowd leaving the woman standing there. He walked into the building and opened a huge door. Instantly a huge applause greeted him.

"Ladies and gentlemen! Our new Carolinadeivid aftershave and the underwear-model Mr. Delta!"

Women screamed hysterically going toward where he was. He blew kisses to all and in turn the cheers and excitement filled the whole conference hall.

A rabbit ran from one edge of the road and stood in the middle of the road chewing grass in its mouth. It stood there for a while before it crossed to the other side of the road. It ran on the well-cut grass before disappearing under a tree. A bird in the tree flew up and high into the sky flying over a huge area of beautiful well-trimmed botanic gardens until it reached a huge mansion below. A car approached from the other side toward the mansion. Inside the car was Victoria, a blonde with a slim body frame and a gorgeous face smartly dressed in a female suit. She looked in the mirror above the inside of the car. She retracted her lips in her mouth and then protracted the lips. She dozed the lips with a clean tissue as the car rolled to the parking area. There were several expensive cars outside. She took her purse and entered the mansion. A woman came to meet her.

"Welcome back Victoria."

"Hello. Thank you for having me."

"This way please."

Even though Victoria was here before maybe a hundred times the place always amazed her. She had always observed the beautiful decorations and paintings. Stacy the house maiden had always moved things around giving the place a new-look feel. She entered the lounge area.

"The place looks different since the last time I was here."

Stacy instantly stopped and walked back. This was her special topic and Victoria knew it.

"Oh, thank you. I changed the theme. This one integrates light colors and is a more relaxed theme. Less detailed items that requires more focus and more flowers and empty spaces. I think this is the best with a lot of people. But surprising the boss does not like this one. He prefers all his special paintings in this room."

"This is beautiful. I love it."

"Okay wait here I will go and tell him that you are here."

Victoria was admiring the lounge decorations when Stacy came back.

"He can see you now. This way please."

Victoria followed through a long corridor. A quick knock on the door before Stacy opened and held the door for Victoria.

"Thank you, Stacy."

Victoria entered a huge study room with books, shelves and more paintings. On one side it had this huge window that faced the other side. The outside scenery was beautiful facing the botanic gardens. She walked to the window and stood at the window. Further was a fishpond. She could hear birds chirping. There was a sharp but short knock on the other inside door before the door swung open.

Dylan entered the study room. Dylan was probably the richest man in the country. He had inherited his father's fortune at a tender age. He was tall, and he wore reading glasses.

"Greetings Sir."

"Victoria, what brings you here?"

She sighed before sitting down. Dylan walked to his desk and sat down.

Victoria leaned forward and looked at Dylan straight into his eyes.

"It's the Leaders, Sir."

Immediately Dylan stood up and walked to the window.

"The Leaders?"

"Yes Sir."

There was silence for a while. He turned around and looked at Victoria.

"What do they want this time? A new loan?"

Victoria did not reply straight away.

"They said they want to meet as soon as possible."

Dylan turned away looking outside the window.

"That's all they have been doing for the past years, meet. I will let them wait this time."

"Sir, I think it's important. They insisted they meet even today if possible."

"I am afraid I cannot offer them another loan if that's what they want."

Victoria stood up and walked toward the window as well.

"They anticipated this reaction from you."

"Really?"

"Yes."

"Fair enough. Thank God they finally came to their senses and realized that I am a very busy man."

"They asked me to tell you that they paid me in advance and generously."

Dylan turned and looked at Victoria.

"Oh, did they? I guess it's time."

That evening a motorcade of SUVs and limousines lined up the road to Dylan's mansion. Dylan looked outside through the bedroom window. He smiled sipping his wine. After a while he heard a huge knock on the door. He did not open but instead shouted something to his wife. A stronghold of twelve men entered the mansion and straight into the study room. In front was Alexander. They took their places among the seats. There was complete silence for a while before Alexander whispered something to Kai. They waited for a long time nearly an hour before Dylan came down. A quick knock and the door opened.

"Gentlemen, Mr. Dylan." shouted Stacy before closing the door behind her.

Dylan did not say a word. He walked to his seat and sat down. Alexander whispered in Kai's ears.

Dylan cleared his throat to speak.

"Gentlemen. Can we proceed with this session?"

He pointed to the space in front of his sofa.

Alexander stood up and looked at Kai and all the Leaders and then at Dylan. He looked at the seat next to Dylan that was empty and looked back at Kai. Kai signaled him to approach him.

"Can we proceed with his wing-man missing?"

"If I remember correctly, no. He or she must be present at the beginning and when we finally claim our Torch back. You know what to do."

"Thank you, Sir, for giving us your time at such short notice. We would like to request that your wing-man be present as well as the matters to be discussed here are of paramount importance."

Dylan sat up straight. He looked around among these men for a while.

"Nothing to be afraid of please proceed. You have my word."

Alexander walked to the center of the study room.

"Thank you, Sir."

Everyone looked at him.

"We are here today to make things right once and for all."

Kai stood up and looked at Dylan.

"Sorry to interrupt. I think we cannot proceed until your wing-man personally over passed his or her right to be present at this meeting. Hugo never gave us that chance and see what happened?"

"I understand but you can continue he will be here."

Alexander walked to Kai.

"I think we can proceed by the time we do the exchange he will be here."

Kai wasn't pleased but anyway he sat down and listen as Alexander delivered his speech.

"We are here to honor our obligations and initiate the exchange proceedings. We are very glad for doing business with you and on behalf of our forefathers we are here to fulfill the promise."

"Hold it!"

Dylan shouted with a strong voice.

Alexander stopped and looked at Dylan then at all the Leaders.

"You can never fulfill the promise. To fulfill the promise means to pay whatever your fathers owed and any interest until the day we return the Torch. We are talking about real money here and without wasting my time can you tell me how much you are willing to pay toward settling."

Alexander looked confused for a while. He threw a quick glance at Kai and the Leaders.

"Yes, Sir we have calculated all what the Torch's value is up to date and that's what we are going to pay you."

"What? Where did you get that kind of money?"

He stood up and looked at Alexander. Instantly the door swung open and everyone looked at Ryan who stood at the door. Ryan was a very huge man with a temper of three lions put together. He was a man of few words and cursing compensated for talking less. He meant business.

He walked slowly and squeezed himself in the sofa.

Dylan whispered in his ears.

"Yes, tell me where you got the money from?"

Alexander tried to explain before Kai interrupted.

"None of your business."

Dylan stared at Ryan who leaned toward him. The

two men whispered among themselves.

"Show us the money first." requested Ryan with a strong voice.

Alexander looked at Kai and then at everyone before going to sit down. The four strong men accompanying him, and the Leaders got up and left the room.

Dylan sat there with his heart in his hands breathing heavily and looking very upset.

The four men returned with huge bags.

Alexander stood up and quickly opened all the bags showing them to Dylan and Ryan.

Dylan and Ryan walked to the center of the room and checked the money. They then walked back to their seats and sat down. Dylan looked like an angry animal. He couldn't speak with rage.

"Can you all excuse us," shouted Ryan.

Alexander looked at Kai who nodded lightly. They started walking out of the study room before Ryan asked Alexander to stay behind on his own.

Alexander stopped and looked at Dylan.

"I am not my father."

The door closed behind them.

Dylan shook with rage.

"Where did they get the money from? All this is my

money."

Ryan looked a little surprised.

"I understand they are giving you all this money shouldn't you be rejoicing boss."

"You don't get it do you?"

"It's still your money."

"This agreement runs back to generations before. It should continue to generations to come. They can never take back the Torch. That Torch had been in our family for generations."

"No problem. Take the money I will deal with them."

A while later the Leaders and Alexander entered back in the study room.

"I have reasons to believe that this money might be stolen money. Fulfilling the promise with stolen money is not what we all have in mind. This does not only invalidate the agreement but make me confiscate the money as well."

Alexander got up shaking with rage.

"Where we get the money from is none of your business, you bastard. You think I don't know that you killed my father. We want our Torch. Take your money and let us be a people again."

Ryan got up and banged the table so hard with the side of his fist. His eyes hard turned red instantly with rage.

Alexander stopped talking instantly.

"Who are you calling a bastard?"

Dylan raised his hand before Ryan sat down.

"We want our Torch within thirty days as agreed."

"Or else what?" asked Ryan clipping his hands together.

"Maybe I strangle you in front of these goners."

Kai got up.

"We came in peace and we shall go in peace."

Dylan signaled them to leave. Dylan and Ryan stood at the window as the motorcade of SUVs and limousines left his property.

"I have failed," suggested Dylan looking sad with a haunted face.

"For generations we have made it difficult for them to have the money. I have invested millions of dollars, putting effective collectors everywhere making sure that no one has enough money even to have a basic normal life let alone to pay the money back. I have failed. I will go down the books as the one who was weak. Imagine the stigma on my kids."

Ryan touched Dylan's shoulder.

"Leave this to me boss. That fool will end up like his father."

"No. First find out how and where they got all this

money from."

"Maybe they are drinking from your well as well?"

Dylan looked lost in thought.

"No, I don't think so. They don't dare."

Detective Braden got out of his car and stood outside checking and scanning the whole area. He was outside a block of flats. They had a huge billboard wall around them and with two narrow gates next to each other one for going in and one for coming out. He removed his sun glasses before walking toward the gates. He walked to the in-gate and as soon as he was at the gate a man bumped into him so hard that he staggered backward. He glanced at the man before the movements of a falling paper caught his attention. The paper fell as if in slow motion dancing until it hits the ground. Detective Braden looked up at the man. He was wearing sun glasses. The detective looked at the man after noticing some strange facial movements but instantly the man knelt and picked up the small torn paper. He walked away.

The detective walked toward the flats. The door entrance to one of the flats looked as if someone had forced in. The detective quickly ran to the gates and looked for the man he had bumped into. He stood at the gates and noticed that the man had come out through the in-gates. He went inside the block of flats and checked all the flats. None of the flats were broken into. He checked and rechecked but he could not tell which flat the man has been. He called for back-up and left someone parked outside.

One beautiful day, it was very sunny and lovely ideally for an outdoor sunbath or nap. Dylan was reading his paper relaxed outside with Ryan and Stacy.

"We can't get rid of everyone. These men represent their clan. Anything that happens to them is likely to stir a revolt something we don't want now."

"You had the same fears before Hugo's task."

"I know. Alexander is likely to stand firm and not cooperate."

"Maybe start with him?"

"We have our money. Maybe hold on to the Torch forever. If I give them the Torch back it means giving them hope and the power for uprising tomorrow and that will be like shooting myself in the foot."

"Boss what's with this Torch I don't get it?"

"Look someone is coming."

"They have come for the Torch. You two go inside I will talk to them on my own."

Stacy and Ryan walked inside the mansion. A red SUV approached driving slowly. Dylan smiled that only a few men had been sent instead of all the delegate. The car came to a halt a few meters from where Dylan was. A man jumped out wearing sunglasses. Dylan just gave him a quick glance and waited for him to come closer.

"Beautiful day!"

"It is that explains me out here otherwise I would be in the study room. Where are the others?"

"Excuse me?"

Dylan sat up straight.

"Who are you?"

"Let's just say your worst nightmare."

"I don't think so," replied Dylan seriously.

"What makes you so sure?"

Ryan opened the door and walked out fast toward Dylan.

"Is this the guy?"

"Whoa! Wait a minute. I am a cop."

"Do you have a search warrant?"

"No."

"So, you have no business being here."

"Don't worry boss he was just leaving."

"Just a few questions and I will be out of here before you know it."

"No."

"Or you prefer talking at the station."

Dylan looked at Ryan.

"I am investigating the bank robberies."

"Okay, I will stop you there. I have nothing to do with that. All my money is legit, but I can give you a name of a person who can help you with that."

The detective looked surprised that he started laughing.

"Nice one. Nice try but no."

"Alexander Hugo. They settled their debt and if you can leave us. Thank you."

The detective typed that and when he had finished, he started walking back to his SUV. He jumped inside and was about to drive off when Dylan shouted. "One thing Detective. When you have the answers, can you let me know where they have found that money."

CHAPTER TEN

Alexander entered the Leaders Compound. This was a huge complex where the Leaders spent their time. They were playing the Seven-stones game. The compound was built around what was once believed to be the last place where the Torch was last used. This was a Holy place to the Leaders. Most of the forefathers were all buried around this place and most of the people had already bought land for their graves here. This was the place where the initial exchange had taken place. He walked to the games compound.

"I heard you are here. How has it been Leader?"

"Oh! Alex nice of you to pay us a visit. What do we owe the pleasure to?"

"Thought I find out how you have been doing? It has been four weeks now."

"Everyone is celebrating. The Leaders are rejoicing that in our time they will unite us again with the Holy Torch. We shall have a blessed life. For generations we failed to perform the ceremonies. Only if you knew how this means to us. When time arrives in old age, you will understand. I just wish your father was here."

"Speaking about my father you never explained what really happened."

Kai moved his piece in the Seven-stones games. He looked at Alexander.

"I think the past is best left alone. Trust me you don't want to know."

Alexander walked toward Kai and looked at him in the eyes.

"You said that if I can find the money, you will tell me when this is over."

Kai just shook his head and played his turn.

"I met my end of the bargain one way or the other you have to do the same."

"We haven't got the Torch yet, I say we wait until we have brought the Torch home. History, they say tends to repeat itself."

The other Leaders agreed by nodding their heads.

"Remember Hugo."

"Listen Kai if you don't tell me now he might play the same game. If I know then I will be in a better position to negotiate."

"The kid has a point," said one of the Leaders.

Alexander got really upset.

"Listen I don't know what you want. Maybe you want this monster to kill me too."

All the Leaders looked at Kai.

"If it was your son standing here today surely you would want him to know. Likewise, I have to know."

Kai got up and started walking out of the Games hall. Alexander stood there looking at Kai as walked out. The other Leaders followed him. The last Leader to leave held the door and waited. Alexander followed him and left the hall. They all walked toward the Holy chamber that once housed the Torch. No one has ever been in this chamber for generations. Kai stood at the door surrounded by the other Leaders. He waited for Alexander to move closer. He put his hand in his clothes and retrieved a huge key.

"I thought you can only enter when we have the Torch." quipped Alexander. The Leaders all looked at him.

"We thought you said you want to know?"

"Yes, but I heard stories about entering this chamber

without the Torch."

"Stories are true."

Kai proceeded to open the door. Alexander's heart beat started beating faster as Kai struggled to open the door. Instantly the sound of something falling inside startled all. Kai pushed the door open.

The chamber was a huge hall with what looked like an altar at the middle. There was a huge pillar in the middle. Surrounding the place were ten stones surrounding the altar. On the other side were stone slabs.

"What is this place I thought this was a place of worship or something."

"Tradition informs us that before we bring the Torch in we have to perform a ceremony to welcome the Torch in for the first time."

"Does tradition say about returning it?"

They all looked at each other.

"The Torch was never to leave this chamber in the first place."

"What? So why did they exchange it for money?"

"Our forefathers settled here first. They established the place as the Holy place. One day they were told that the land had been sold and bought, and that they had to move," said the Leader Zack.

"Yes, I am listening."

"They refused to move. They fought back but their leader was killed and died there. After his death the supposedly new owners then agreed that if they are to stay they would pay him for staying there. This was paying for the whole clan over years. In the end they could not pay up."

"So, they took the Torch?"

"Correct? The book as well which was written by the original Leaders."

"Okay what about my father?"

Zack pointed at the seats and everyone sat down surrounding the pillar and the altar.

"Your father died in here on that altar."

"What! You killed my father?"

"No. It was not us."

Alexander fumed with anger.

"I thought you said it was Dylan's men?"

"Yes, they call them the New World Leaders."

"In the Torch Book it is written that where the Torch is the people have to establish the Leaders who will look after the Torch and perform rituals."

Alexander got up and walked toward the altar.

"So, are you saying that these new Leaders sacrificed my father? Why?"

"You have to understand that long time ago things

were different. The Torch Book declared death as a sacrifice to anyone who traded the Torch for money.”

“Let me get this straight are you saying that my father took a loan against the Torch and then failed to pay back?”

“He never got the money in the first place.”

Kai looked at Alex.

“The exchange always happens in the Torch Chamber. They led your father in here. Instead of giving him the extra loan they attacked him and placed him on the altar.”

“So, it’s true what I heard?”

They all looked down.

He clenched his fists and shook with rage.

“They cut him to pieces while he was still alive. Removing body parts until he died.”

Alexander cried in anguish.

They all looked at him with wide-opened eyes. He instantly stopped crying and looked at them surprised.

“What?”

He thought for a while and walked away from the altar.

“Are you fucking crazy!” he shouted.

“You have two days left to bring the Torch or else we have to sacrifice you too as in the book.”

"Let's go and get the Torch. He said that we can collect after thirty days."

"He lied. You must collect the Torch within thirty days. Two more days left."

"What? Let's go at once."

"Oh no. You forced us in here we can never leave the Torch Chamber until the Torch is back. I guess you are on your own. Once we have entered the Torch Chamber without the Torch, we can never leave."

Alexander smiled for a split second.

"I will not come back if I can't get it. I paid the money you all saw it. What can you do?"

Kai smiled sarcastically.

"If we can't do it Dylan had been preparing for the past twenty-eight days. He owns the Torch it's his duty to eliminate you,"

"Damn it! If I didn't insist on knowing when were you going to tell me all this?"

"I thought I explained from day one that that's how your father lost his life. We expected you to show power and to refuse to leave without the Torch."

"So, you tricked me into joining the Leaders?"

The all looked at each other.

"Even then why a young man like you would want to join the Leaders."

"What?"

"You were supposed to run away and refuse. You should have let us die with your father. We set your father up indirectly. We were supposed to go with him. All of us, we are all equal and there can't be a leader. We are all equal parts of a whole, without one we cease to exist."

Alexander pulled the gun and pointed at Kai.

"Why did you choose me to be your leader in the first place?"

Kai remained silent, he looked at the others.

"Damn it! Tell me before I shoot all of you."

"Go ahead, better die this way than to die like your father."

Alexander felt a lump in his heart choking him.

He cocked up the gun and aimed at Kai.

"Come on talk! Talk now before I shoot you!" shouted Alexander waving the gun at all of them.

"You don't want to talk? Okay."

He put the gun on Kai's forehead.

"Okay. Okay don't shoot I will talk."

Delta got out of his car and walked fast into the huge mall in the city. He spoke briefly on the phone before cursing. He wore his sunglasses. Across the road was a lady who was sitting outside looking everywhere.

She looked at him as he cursed and started laughing before Delta disappeared inside. He went inside the Carolinadeivid shop. He removed his shoes and trousers leaving him in the Carolinadeivid briefs. He removed his shirt leaving him with a gold necklace with the initials KD. He pushed his hair backward and squinted his eyes and smiled looking in the mirror. Instantly his phone started ringing. He answered it and started talking.

"How come you are late? You know I can't wait. If you are not here in twenty minutes, I am out."

He walked outside the shop.

"You fucking mad or what forty minutes? I am going."

He swerved, and the gold necklace swerved as well. A few people started gathering outside mostly ladies and women starring at him.

One lady walked to him and hugged him and took a selfie with him. One after the other they all surrounded him taking selfies with him.

The guard from the other shop approached him.

"This is a mall and not some massage parlor."

"Oh no. No! I am an Underwear-model."

Detective Braden had just entered the mall when he heard the commotion. A lot of people now were going up the mall to the Carolinadeivid shop. The detective laughed as well but somehow stood still on the moving elevator the moment he saw Delta talking on the phone. Instincts kicked in. He put his hand on his gun and waited until he was near. The lifts door suddenly opened, Rex and Julie walked out of the lift. Instantly Delta lowered the hand that was holding the cellphone and started walking toward them. Julie covered her mouth and giggled at his sight.

"It worked I told you it will work."

Instantly the detective touched Delta's shoulder with the other hand holding his gun but still in its pocket clipped on his belt.

Delta turned and saw the detective.

The detective gobsmacked by his looks stared at him with the hand on his gun trying to picture if they had met before.

"Don't worry I get that a lot. Just last week this woman thought that she had seen an angel."

Everyone laughed, and the ladies cheered on.

"Oh, put that away no need for a real gun Detective."

The crowd went berserk. The women cheered on and applauded looking at his briefs.

He hugged the detective looking at the crowd.

"I am an Underwear-model Detective, I am Delta."

Embarrassed the detective looked at the crowd and walked away. Soon after Delta, Rex and Julie entered the Carolinadeivid shop and began the photo-shoot.

The detective walked in and glanced at him briefly. Somehow, he felt like they have met before.

"Don't shoot I don't have a gun!" shouted Delta raising his hands. The crowd applauded hysterically. The photographer laughed as well. The crowd loved his jokes and charm. The detective looked at him with evil eyes. He smiled and for a split second his face twitched like a raged lion's. The detective looked closely and instantly his face looked at peace and like an angel's. Instantly the detective walked out of the shop.

"Great! Bravo! I love it. Everyone loved every bit. Look how the shop is now full of people. Now I will let the video-crew do what they do best and you I don't think I have to say anything."

A group of women have gathered around him with the shop's magazines in their hands. He signed the magazines which had his photo on.

"I love this job."

"You can write down your number as well." shouted one woman.

Julie walked closer.

"No cellphone numbers. He is already taken."

"By who?" everyone shouted.

Julie pointed to a woman in the corner near the entrance who happened to be the store manager as well. A lady by the name of Charlotte. Delta stopped signing and looked in that direction with admiration.

They all looked at this Charlotte. Their faces had this doubtful expression written all over their face that that was not true. A gorgeous sexy lady had just walked in and was walking toward him. It clicked to most, as the lady flirtatiously started doing her hair touching it flirtatiously and sexily.

"Ah!" sighed the crowd.

She looked at him and at his briefs and started giggling at the same time crying tears of joy.

Delta's face moved quickly like an angry animal's about to attack for a split second but enough for her to have seen that. His face had creased as well with rage. She blinked but looked backward. She looked at Delta and then at the other woman. She stopped and looked at the woman. The following woman looked at the full view and saw Delta in his briefs she forced to hold a laugh.

"Don't be shy come," said Delta looking at the first lady.

She blushed as he hugged her.

"Underwear-model?"

Delta just opened his arms with a genuine smile on his face. The other woman arrived.

"Ah it's you. I didn't notice."

"Have we met before?"

The woman looked at the lady Delta was hugging.

"The woman driver?" said Eva as she recognized the woman from the other day.

"Can you sign this for me please," asked Detective Kristy.

"Can we talk after?" she added dressed in civilian clothes.

"If you can wait after the video shoot maybe yes."

"I can't wait. You know what? I will give you my number when you are free call me okay," said Detective Kristy writing down her cellphone number. She tore a piece of paper and when she was about to hand the paper to Delta she dropped it and looked at Delta. She walked close to him and started writing the number on his bare chest looking at him straight in his eyes. Eva looked at Delta's face and opened her eyes in shock.

"I don't think it's a good idea. He is not interested."

Delta put on an angel face and smiled. The detective started walking away. She stopped and looked at his briefs she smiled and walked out of the shop.

Eva stayed with him throughout the video shoot.

"Let's say this is our second date. I will call you okay."

"I want to go with you."

"I can't we just met besides I am very busy."

She looked at his chest and started rubbing off the

number written there by the detective.

"No. No. No. I want this number."

"I knew it. Just pushing me away before we even started. Don't call me!" she walked out.

"Julie check!" shouted Delta.

Julie went to look if she had gone.

She noticed that she stopped and looked back to see if he was following before disappearing.

"You were brilliant," shouted Rex.

"We have done it. You know what that means?" continued Rex.

"Partying!" he shouted.

"I can't this week."

"Running home for sex. I can't blame you. Imagine stripping for all those women and fail to nail even one."

"Welcome to the world of super models."

"Who is the new lady?"

"Let's just say a friend of a friend."

Detective Braden ran to the corner of the road and looked. There was no one. He ran to the other end and looked but the road was empty. He run back into the block of flats. He pulled his gun and stealthily searched for the flat that had been broken into. He had tried to open the door but had found out that all the doors were locked. He got into the lift that took him to the upper level. Stealthily with a gun pointing everywhere he reached a door that had been forced open. He slid the door open, peeped inside before going inside. He aimed the gun everywhere and entered inside the flat. He checked all the rooms, but the flat was empty. He entered the bedroom and opened the drawer instantly one of the letters caught his attention. The piece of paper with the address and name of the recipient had been torn off. He checked the addresses on the other letters. He noticed that all the letters were for that flat. He quickly went downstairs in the lounge and was about to go out of the flat when instantly a shadow appeared at the door. He froze with fear. Instantly he felt the cold barrel of the gun touching his forehead.

"Drop the gun!"

The man was wearing sunglasses. His face started moving, shaking as if an animal about to attack. He heard the cocking up of the gun. His heart beat elevated. Sweat droplets drenched down his neck. He could feel the droplets trickling down his belly.

"Don't shoot!"

"I have heard that before."

"Ah!"

A loud screamed woke up Rose.

"He shot me!"

"Who shot you? What is it darling? You are having a nightmare."

Detective Braden looked at his girlfriend sweat droplets trickling down his forehead.

A motorcade arrived outside the huge building in the city. Quickly Oliver got out. At the same time three men and a woman got out from the other SUVs and followed behind Oliver. One of the men stayed at the entrance, the other at the first floor, the other two went all the way with Oliver to the fifth floor. They stayed outside a huge wooden double door. Oliver entered inside. The office was gigantic. Everything inside was all in dark wood giving the office the dark theme. On the other sides were two huge windows that helped lighten the room. The outside views were magnificent. In the middle was a huge wooden polished desk. There was a huge glass cabinet that housed a huge collection of trophies and memorabilia. A woman in her sixties stood at the huge window. She acted as if she didn't hear Oliver come in.

"The view is out of this world. I travel in a world of my own. Come and see."

Oliver reluctantly walked toward the woman and stood next to her. She didn't look at him but instead remained focused outside.

"They say what goes around comes around. There is a lot of truth in that. Do you agree?"

Oliver tried to control his anger and sounded calm.

"To me it doesn't come very fast enough than it should."

"Patience Oli. These things take time."

"How many more years? It has been more than seventeen years now."

The woman looked calm and seemed unconcerned at all.

"Everything is going according to plan."

"What plan is that? You mean wait until when everyone has forgotten and too old to do anything about this?"

"We have started the transition phase. We have put people who want to fight your cause as well. We need common agreement for the plan to work. Look all around you. Everyone now is a trigger, a catalyst, an advocate you name it. A lot of time, money and sweat has gone into this project."

"As far as I am concerned it's not fast enough."

"You think I spend my time admiring the views. Right?"

The woman walked to the comfy sofa and sat down.

"Don't get me wrong nothing personal. I don't see what you are waiting for."

"Please sit down."

Oliver instantly turned and walked toward the sofa.

"It's not easy you know. We must convince everyone concerned. Some people still are objecting to that preferring that nothing is done in our time."

"Who are they and why?"

"The world is not as easy as you think. Not everyone lost their loved ones. Some got a huge bung instead."

Oliver instantly got up and walked toward the window hiding his anguish at hearing that.

"What's the way forward."

"We have to wait. Most have cited lack of jurisdiction to interfere."

"Who has jurisdiction then? If you can't do anything who will then?"

"People prefer to forget and move on."

"My family, my son, my daughter, and my wife all perished needlessly. Who will be hold accountable for that?"

"No matter how you want to look at it in the end it becomes a personal matter."

The woman walked to the window as silence broke out briefly.

"If you wait for a collected decision you are looking at ten to twenty more years. Every day that passes by they are getting stronger as well using any means possible. The world is not equipped to deal with war crimes and crimes against humanity at such magnitude."

"So, you are saying we let these monsters get away with murder?"

The woman did not reply but simply looked outside the window.

"Who can help?"

The woman breathed heavily and looked at Oliver.

Oliver left the huge building. He stood outside and looked at the tall building and in the office which he was in. He saw the woman stood at the window looking at him. He jumped in the SUV and the motorcade left.

Wynne a heavily built man with a burr cut and hooded eyes looked at Paige before looking in the rear-view mirror.

"I think we have company."

Paige, with short blonde hair of medium built in her mid-thirties looked in the rear-view mirror as well. Instantly she took out her gun and checked the bullets cartridge.

"Alert! We have company."

Enzo looked in the rear-view mirror.

"Boss we have company hold on tight."

Oliver looked surprised.

A huge SUV approached very fast and plowed at the back of the car driven by Wynne. The car swerved but Wynne gained control. He pushed the horn button and Enzo stepped on the gas. Wynne looked in the rear-view mirror and noticed that two other SUVs were behind the other SUV.

Enzo instructed the driver to drive faster. Paige fired shots through the side window. The SUV pulled back briefly before speeding up and scattering bullets shattering the back-window screen. Wynne and Paige ducked and briefly lost control of the car. Paige rolled to the back seat and fired shots. The bullets only managed to leave cracks on the screen.

"Bulletproof!" she shouted looking at Wynne. She rolled back to the front seat.

"Better step on the gas pedal."

Wynne gave Paige a quick glance and drove like a rally driver swerving sometimes to avoid the flying bullets, the cars screeched tires as the chase continued.

"I will try to hold them back. Take the boss to safety." said Wynne over the phone looking at Paige.

Paige folded her lips in disapproval.

"Are you trying to get us killed?"

Wynne did not reply.

Oliver looked scared and haunted. The ringing cellphone startled him. Enzo looked at Oliver.

"Don't answer it."

"I have to answer it," replied Oliver.

"Yes. We are being attacked!"

The woman laughed softly.

"Can you send back-up? We are heading along…"

Oliver looked at Enzo and looked at the screen of the cellphone.

"Hello, are you still there?"

"Yes Oliver."

Oliver felt hopeless and betrayed.

"Did you send them?"

"You don't understand…"

"But why? I asked for your help."

"You will destroy everything just to revenge your wife and kids?"

"So, it was you all along? All the attempts on my life…"

The woman remained quiet.

A huge fireball engulfed Wynne and Paige's car.

Enzo and Oliver and the driver looked in the rear-view mirrors helplessly. Oliver placed the phone down. They could still hear a woman's voice talking. Oliver looked at Enzo as the following SUVs passed by the sides of the burning car and approached at high speed.

"Take this you might need it."

Enzo handed a gun to Oliver. The two men looked at each other before bullets sounds sends them ducking.

CHAPTER ELEVEN

Detective Braden looked around at the traffic light. He saw a huge billboard with Delta in his briefs. He thought for a while. He remembered the day he bumped into someone like him at the block of flats. He had this nagging feeling that it was him. As far as he knows he was clean. He had checked him. He also remembered the nightmare he had. It was still vivid that he felt a cold feeling run down his spine. He thought about Dylan too. There was something about him too. The fact that he admitted receiving loads of money raised more questions than answers. There was only one way to find out. Alexander angrily looked at the Leaders. He felt that they knew more than they were telling him. He realized that they might have betrayed his father than they were admitting.

"I will be back I am going to collect the Torch."

They all looked at each other.

"You all be better be here when I come back,"

He walked out and closed the door behind him. He jumped into his car and drove off the compound. The moment his car left, Detective Braden's car was just entering the compound. He caught a quick glimpse of the driver. He stopped the car but then continued to the reception. There was no one. He looked around. He went to the games hall. There was an abandoned game. He stopped and looked around. He remembered someone telling him that the Leaders never left a game unfinished. He walked to the conference hall. The hall was empty. There were people coming and going on the other side. He walked there. There was a huge church. He entered inside and looked at everyone. He walked out and was about to leave when he threw a quick glance toward the Torch Hall. He dismissed the idea and drove off in the direction the other car had gone.

Alexander drove fast changing gears quickly the more he thought about how his father had died. He felt cheated somehow. Joining the Leaders had given him some sense of comfort over his death as he took his seat among his friends. These Leaders have given him some sense of resolve. He had pressed hard to get the money to end this once and for all. He felt even more betrayed as he thought about Dylan. He opened the glove compartment and looked for the spare gun. His car hit a hump before flying into the air. It bumped in the road sending fire sparks everywhere. Dylan looked outside the window and breathed heavily. Alexander's car entered Dylan's yard to the mansion. He parked his car and stood outside for a while. He noticed Dylan standing at the window. A strange feeling trickled down his spine and his body. He remembered his father when he was a boy. Instantly he walked like a soldier, fast and straight. Stacy opened the door without saying anything. Alexander went straight to the study room and entered inside.

Dylan was there in his sofa.

"You don't give up do you?"

Alexander looked around first before sitting down.

"I am here to collect the Torch better be fast they are waiting."

"They, who?" asked Dylan sarcastically.

"The Leaders of course."

Dylan stood up and walked to the window.

"Do you know what happened the day your father died?"

"Don't waste my time. They told me. The Torch?"

Dylan looked at Alexander.

"Did they? I don't believe you."

"The Torch?"

"I am just saying I don't believe they would tell you that they traded your father for this money."

Alexander felt angry.

"You are lying bastard. It was you who got my father killed."

Dylan walked to his sofa and sat down.

"Your father was very stupid just like you."

Alexander instantly got up.

"Stop insulting my father."

"The others choose money in perpetuity and handed him in and the Torch."

"You robbed them, and you have never given them the money."

"I promised them a lump sum in the end and thanks to you it came sooner than I thought."

"I don't care. I just need the Torch. We have to fulfill the book."

Dylan stood up again and walked to the window. He admired the view before looking at Alexander.

"You don't get it do you? The Torch is mine without the Torch no one will listen to me. I keep the Torch, everyone worships me. I keep the Torch I control everyone. I keep the Torch everyone pays me protection money even the banks."

"Nonsense! The Torch is for our clan. People are paying you money, so they can get the Torch back."

"Either way I am saying it's a money maker to me. Look how easy you got all that money? Do you think the bank would have offered you that kind of money if you didn't have the Torch? I worked very hard to put all those bank CEOs where they are. I knew it that to make money was to put people who truly believe in the Torch and what it stands for."

Alexander sat down.

"You can't stand the truth! Your father died for something he believed in."

Alexander stood up instantly.

"I said stop insulting my father!"

"Or else what? Want to shoot me?"

"The cops will deal with you. You son of a beast! I have a clan to lead. I don't want your blood on my hands."

Dylan started laughing.

"Funny I gave them your name. I bet they are coming here right now for you."

"What for?"

"Bastard! You don't know? Bank robbery."

"Who will believe that? They all know it was a collection."

"I don't think so. See like I said. The CEOs who gave you this money work for me."

"You son of a beast! My money is clean. They will keep the Torch."

"Let me tell you something you don't know. The whole world revolves around this. This is more than you can handle. Listen to me very carefully. The bank declared this money stolen already. Do you think they will give you that money for this Torch?"

"Why not? If it means nothing to you why are you keeping it then? To us this is more than just a Torch. To us this symbolizes freedom. It reminds us of courage. It remains us of the brave people of our clan who died standing for us. It means freedom of all future generations. If it means going to war with you and all these crooks so be it."

Dylan laughed. He clapped hands.

"What a moving speech. Just like your father. Stubborn. Maybe I kill you too."

Alexander pulled his gun.

"I don't want to kill you. I want you to die the same way as my father. The Leaders are waiting for the Torch and the sacrifice. I left them in the Torch Chamber."

Dylan for the first time looked scared or it appears so to Alexander.

"Funny you said that."

"Why is that?"

"My people are ready too for a sacrifice."

Instantly the door opened. Ryan and eleven more people covered in gowns came out all holding guns aimed at Alexander.

Instantly the table started opening, converting to an altar. The pillar opened like flower petals blossoming to reveal a golden Torch with diamonds and minerals around it. It glittered brightly shining in the room. The windows automatically closed giving the room a dark feel. Alexander froze for a while. He tried to grab Dylan, but Ryan was very fast to react. Alexander lay down on the floor bleeding. When he woke up he was tied onto the altar. He opened his eyes but the rays of the golden Torch with all the glittering diamonds blinded him. He turned his head and saw Dylan dressed up in a gown as well.

"Untie me right now!" he shouted trying to free himself.

"If I don't go back with the Torch, the Leaders are going to inform the police," he struggled very hard to free himself.

"What Leaders?"

Alexander looked at Dylan.

"They traded you for the money."

"The police?"

Dylan lifted his head and one of the people in there switched on the huge screen above the altar. Alexander looked around before watching. He watched a secret recording of detectives Braden and Kristy wearing the gowns too. He looked around in shock.

"Dirty cops. But why?"

"You think that's a coincidence that banks are being robbed in broad-light? It's either ride or die. You chose to die. Just like your father. He had the guts to come here alone. The Leaders stayed away and waited for his death, so that they can get their cut, I mean their share of the money. Likewise, they are waiting too to get their share and witness your death via video streaming."

Delta entered the huge building swiftly wearing sunglasses. He looked at the elevators before he felt someone touching his shoulder. He looked at him.

"Don't touch me."

"Sign in. Who are you visiting?"

"Getting laid here today."

He removed his glasses and looked at the guard.

"Whatever. Just sign in."

He scribbled very fast that even the guard couldn't read.

"Just the looks you can't even write." scorned the

guard.

Delta entered the elevators and selected the floor number twenty where there were residential premises. The guard looked-on and waited for the lift to go up. Delta felt agitated and kicked the lift. He looked around and notice a red-light flashing. He got out at floor twenty.

Delta knocked the door and tried to open the door.

"Who is it?"

"It's me you requested for me!" shouted Delta.

He heard a click sound and opened the door.

Inside was a lady who stood at the window.

"You called for me. I am here."

The woman turned around.

"I don't recall. What do you do?"

"Mail-model."

"Mail-model I never heard of such a thing. Do you mean male-model?"

"I read mails of helpless people around the world seeking help with no answers. I read everyone's pain. I feel the pain of all the people you killed. I feel all your evil."

Delta removed his sunglasses and started shaking like an animal about to maul someone.

"I am sure I did not call you."

"You did. The day you played God. The day you abused. The day you stole. The day you killed. Even just now I can feel a man's feelings of anguish. I can read his mail he sent seeking help and resolve from you. I can even feel his pain the day he died. So, don't say you did not call me."

The woman reached for her table and was about to press the button underneath the table when Delta looked at her.

"It's funny I can feel your call for help even now. Only that it's coming from hell!"

Delta instantly pulled his gun and shot the woman several times. He relaxed and walked out into the lift and down. The guard looked at him.

"I thought you went to floor twenty you just came from floor five."

He leaned very closer to the guard.

"I don't usually do grannies. Our secret."

He winked at the guard and left.

The guard looked confused he sat there for a split second before he followed him.

"Stop there come back here!"

The time he went out Delta's car had already made a U-turn and sped off. The guard went back in running. He took the elevators and straight to level five. There was only one lady he knew on level five. He pushed the door holding his gun. The sight of a young lady standing at the window instantly caught his attention. She stood at the window looking outside.

"Who are you?"

"The Underwear-model?"

"Where is..."

He didn't finish talking, he aimed his gun at her.

"Put your hands up!"

"I found her like that a man had just left."

The guard lowered the gun and entered to check if she was still breathing.

He looked up to talk to the Underwear-model when he felt the barrel of the gun on his forehead.

"Underwear-model. I am taking you down too."

The guard slumped down next to the woman with blood oozing out from his forehead.

CHAPTER TWELVE

The Presidential motorcade arrived outside Tomorrow's World Order's offices. The doors of the limousine swung open. The President Mr. David got out and looked around waving at the crowd that had gathered outside. There were cheers and applause everywhere.

"It starts today! We shall build a new order starting today!"

The crowd went berserk applauding.

"We shall act like superior human beings the way nature intended."

The crowd cheered and clapped hands even louder.

"Today's leaders have backtracked."

He paused and looked at the crowd as they cheered

further.

"Today's environment is not suitable for human life."

"To hell with them!" shouted the crowd.

"Today's leaders have taken the easy route!"

"To hell with them! Our Future Our Say!" shouted the crowd even louder

He stopped and looked at the crowd who kept cheering on hysterically.

"Today's leaders have chosen evil in order to create jobs and fulfill party manifestos!"

He paused for a while. The crowd clapped hands and cheered.

"But we shall act like superior human beings and put the world's resources to better use!"

"Ladies and gentlemen, boys and girls the system has gone bonkers. Billions of dollars are being spent on weapons and digital-agents while the taxpayer has been stripped off any disposal income. Today's leaders are robbing everyone so that they make weapons and digital or viral agents. I say Tomorrow's World Order is the way forward. Our hospitals rely on $billions worth of digitally-man-made agents to function properly. That's bonkers! That's backtracking no matter what angle you want to look at it. They are taking us back to the medieval times when there were no advances in medicine or technology. Today's leaders are reversing previous achievements taking the easy route to create jobs."

The crowd applauded.

"I say no to inferior thinking! 2000 years has passed still we only live up to 80 years on average. If animals can live up to 200 years, why can't we? I am saying there are areas that can create jobs that have not been fully explored. 2000 years have passed yet we rely heavily on fossil fuels. There are areas that need more funding that can create jobs. Today's leaders have emphasized future plans neglecting today's issues. I am not saying it's wrong to focus on the future. I am saying a baby can only walk after crawling. Likewise, basic needs first before fancy weaponry. Our heroes have nowhere to sleep yet we build $ billions worth of weaponry. Countries are getting into debt spending $billions on weaponry. Today's leaders have broken all human rights laws. Today's leaders are inferior in that they see boundaries and differences. They are selfish and therefore ignore the advantages of networking and international cooperation. Communication is a skill taken for granted."

The crowd clapped hands.

"Today I stand here and say that for the past thirty years we have spent nearly $35 trillion making weapons and on military. We collected the world's resources and made the best arsenal which thanks to violations of human rights laws now we can use them. I therefore as the President give way for Directive

Seventeen. Ladies and gentlemen, I declare war to all countries violating human rights laws and to those who are still oppressing others even if that means world war three so be it."

The crowd applauded and cheered.

"It's time. It's showdown!"

"That's right. Give us the chance to see who the real-world leader is."

"Who has the big guns?" shouted one member from the crowd.

All over the world people watched on television. While in neighboring country. President Camden got up.

"He has a point. That's the way forward. Until we destroy all this arsenal, we will never change. We can keep on waging war with third world countries and stealing from them. Let's see who really has the big guns among ourselves."

Vice President Patrick stood up.

"You must be mad. You listen to that warmonger? War destroys life. What good can come out of a war?"

"Listen to yourself. He is a visionary. Greater thinking requires shifting from defense-based economies to economies that are proactive, and which put emphasis more on research and development. We must destroy all the arsenal stockpiles. A new beginning does not come easy or cheap."

"Get him on the phone right now."

Later.

"Mr. President war does not achieve anything."

President David sighed.

"Do you know that for the past 20 years globally we spent nearly $35 trillion on weapons and military?"

"Don't forget we created jobs and met our party goals."

"But you also agree that you have homeless ex-soldiers?"

"That has nothing to do with this."

"The years after the war are the best years in terms of peace and global cooperation. Look at all the treaties that brought nations together they were all only signed after the war. After wars humanity don't see differences. We don't see boundaries. We work together for the common good. We cooperate. We spend money on space travel. We spend money on other things other than weapons. Today's leaders are backtracking. Tomorrow's World Order is now the overseer of all world countries. Now. It's either you are on our side. The law-abiding ones, the ones who foster human development. Or you are on the inferior side. You still see differences. You are still making digital-viral-agents and use them on your own people as well. Or you reverse all previous achievements to satisfy short-term goals. In that case

Directive Seventeen is meant for you and you shall feel the full force. Good bye."

The line went dead.

"Darling why war? For years all these world leaders have avoided wars. What makes you different?"

The President hugged his wife and kissed her.

"My love, for over 2000 years humanity is still going the same road with the same results."

"People stick to the tried and trusted. This has worked okay?"

"You can say that, but we are not living to our full potential. God created a superior human being. Do you think this is what God intended?"

There was silence for a while.

"I think God gave use the power to communicate. Unlike animals we can all talk and learn. That separates us from animals. But if animals can outsmart humans; living up to 200 years then it does not make any sense. Today's leaders would rather make a strong viral strain and wipe out populations. But I think a superior mind will look for new alternatives. Human instincts. When your family grows bigger, you don't look for a strong viral strain to wipe out others but instead you look for a bigger house and relocate. Correct?"

"Correct."

"Globally why can't we do the same?"

"That can't be the reason to kill millions."

The President sat down.

"Okay, you got me there."

"Today's environment is not ideal for human life. Too much harmful digital-viral-man-made-agents. I like the way God created us. I dislike these fake gods who think they can control and change humanity. I long for a new beginning the way God intended but first we must clean this mess. Eliminate all weapons. Eliminate all these digital-agents. They are based on viral mutations therefore not good to human life. After the war, everything will have been destroyed. This time we put new laws of what people can do and cannot do. No reversing of previous achievements. The world should be one. We shall spend money building roads, networks, looking for new sources of energy, new accommodation maybe in Mars or some other planet. Do you think it's fair to see early aging, early wrinkles, unknown diseases and all that? No funding for those who make harmful digital-agents. Destroy these evil people first. That way we have smart and hardworking citizens. This gives me also the chance to eliminate all inferior thinking and evil people. Speaking of which; where is Delta the Assassin?"

CHAPTER THIRTEEN

Delta entered a huge building outside the city. He walked inside looking everywhere. He took the long corridor that lead him to the reception.

"I need to see the CEO of the bank."

"Mr. Kyle is in his office are you the model?"

"Yes, madam."

"He is expecting you."

Delta smiled and walked in style going to the elevators. He smiled and straightened his suit. He knocked at the door and waited to be invited in. Mr. Kyle did not hesitate. He immediately answered the door inviting Delta in. He smiled and entered the office.

"What can I do for you Mr. Delta?"

"I want to do business with the bank, but my main concerns are with how secure these banks are especially with the past month's bank robberies."

"We were unfortunate to be targeted but I am glad to say that we have improved greatly in that area."

"What do you say to the fact that some are saying that they were collections rather than bank robberies?"

"People say a lot of things when something goes wrong."

"Mr. Kyle do you pay protection money to anyone? Is someone blackmailing you?"

"Mr. Delta. I think these questions are best asked by someone's else rather than you."

"Did the bank hire a hit-man to kill anyone who investigates this?"

"Mr. Delta are you sure you want to do business with us? Is this a stunt of some kind?"

Delta stood up and walked toward the trophy cabinet.

"I want to be sure that I can trust this bank before I invest my money."

"You sound like you are going to invest billions of dollars. Are you?"

Delta laughed.

"Not really. Thank you for your time."

Delta stood up and started walking toward the door. He opened the door and when he was about to leave when he came back in.

"Mr. Kyle do you believe in the Torch?"

"I am a scientist I believe in facts not myths or any fancy thinking."

Delta walked back in and looked at the pictures on the wall before leaving.

Hailey walked in the digital lab. She looked at the computer that was running a program.

'Conversion completed, storing the digital factor.'

She looked everywhere and observed people who had cables attached to their bodies and hooked to the to the computers in the big hall with the glass walls. She looked again, and this time saw a handsome man standing outside the lab looking inside. He signaled pointing to the door.

Hailey opened the door.

"Hey, should you be here?"

"They say curiosity killed the cat."

"What's all this?"

"Okay come in."

Hailey showed great excitement when given the chance to share the great news with Delta.

"We are capturing feelings all kinds, pain, happiness

and movements and converting these into stored digital versions that can be sold and be bought. Imagine going to the shop to buy an orgasm."

"Hey sorry I am not into this digital stuff."

"What? Get out of here. This is the way forward. This is the future. Imagine being able to walk in a shop and buy a good state of mind. Imagine being able to go in the shop and buy laughter. In case no one is there to tell you a joke you can just buy a laughter to a joke. This is the thing."

"This is not for the youth, right? In other words, your target is the older generation with higher savings. Right?"

"Sure, most of our work is to convert aging features into swap-able digital items. We are capturing youthful features and converting and storing these. In the future the old will be able to go to a supermarket and buy wrinkle free converted digital factor. This will ideally be able to reverse aging."

Delta looked at Hailey whilst listening very attentively.

"It is true also that you are actually capturing and storing ways of making the youth age very fast."

"Not here but it's possible."

"So, you would agree with me that there are high rates of early aging than normal. Would that have anything to do with the research going on here?"

"My area of expertise is capturing digital feelings and

converting these into items that can be bought."

"But there are huge chances that this can be used to control and blackmail people if it falls in the wrong hands?"

"Yes, in the wrong hands sure."

"What is with those people sleeping in there?"

"In order for this to work they have to spend some time sleeping to help the rejuvenation process. They are reversing the effects of old aging."

"I have a question. Is it also true that you can subjugate the feelings to someone else? I am asking if it is possible to 'enslave' someone else."

"I would not use that word, but a similar process is possible. Take the old for example. We can transfer the body or state of mind say pain or feelings from them to the younger ones. The younger ones ought to be less mobile."

"You mean sleeping all the time or even dead?"

"Mr. Delta. You sound like an interrogating officer rather than someone who want to learn."

"Are you saying that this would benefit the old population especially if the subjugating subject is immobile and or dead?"

"In theory yes."

"Could this also explain why one would wage war to kill women and children?"

"Mr. Delta. It's not that easy. The young ones and the women have to have the proper implants for that process to occur."

"You mean they have to have a medical operation done or a vaccine done that injects the implant that will enable all this?"

"Ideally yes, to be precise they need an IMD that can enable the capturing and conversion."

"And this IMD is cheap and easy to implant that this can be done on a large scale? Correct?"

"True, nowadays they manufacture billions of these at minimum unit cost of cents and you can buy them cheaper. The procedure is simply. A pallet gun can be used to inject the IMD the size of a grain of rice, or simply this can be implanted on the lumbar bone."

Delta retrieved a rolled paper being held with a string. He rolled it open. He looked at it.

"Hailey. Hailey Rinks?"

"Yes, that's me."

Delta took a camera and attached it to the gun.

"Sorry you are on me To-do-list."

"No. There must be a mistake. No don't kill me!"

He raised his hand and pulled the trigger. At the same time taking a picture showing the time and the date.

CHAPTER FOURTEEN

"The whole system is corrupt. Over the years they have mastered the art of concealment and dirty tricks. All these institutions are not fit for the purpose. They are there and were all established by the same people we are trying to bring to justice. They are dependent on funding from the very people that we are saying they have fallen below standard. They rely on bungs from the very people we want to face crimes against humanity. We have therefore nominated Tomorrow's World Order as the overseer and leader of all countries until that time when we shall establish a proper establishment that will deal effectively with crimes against humanity at this magnitude," said Delta addressing the international community. There were objections at first but when the leader of

Tomorrow's World Order stood up to address the people they started clapping hands slowly with the noise gradually increasing the more he spoke his views.

Detective Kristy walked to the huge mirrors in her bathroom. She raised a glass of wine and toasted to herself. She smiled and unfastened her hair. She shook her head until all her hair covered her head. She moved closer to the mirror and looked at her beautiful gray eyes. She smiled again and placed the wine glass down. She removed her gown revealing her beautifully shaped and well-toned body. She checked her assets and smiled even further. She walked to the tub and sunk inside the soapy and foamy water. She opened the tap letting the warm water hit her between her legs. She sighed with every pouncing. Slowly she started dosing off in the tub. A car drove slowly around the suburbs. Inside was Delta listening to the Elinadeivid song titled Twenty-three reasons to fall in love.

You are on my To-do-list

I have every reason to do the job and trust me they all say I am good at it

But something about you gives me Twenty-three reasons to love you I don't want to fall in love

Even if I try it will never work between us I have a job to do Like I said you are on my To-do-list

Somehow, I find myself with twenty-three reasons to fall in love

I got to do you

Got to do what I do best Still,

I find twenty-three reasons to fall in love with you.

Delta stopped the car and walked to one of the houses. The lights were on. He stealthily walked to the window and peeped inside. He walked to the front door and tried to open the door. The door was not locked. He noticed the wine bottle on the table in the lounge. He smiled and shoved his gun behind his back-belt and hopped as he removed his shoes one by one then his socks. Then he unfastened the trousers' belt and let his trousers slip down. The gun dropped too startling him. He stopped and listened. He pulled off the Carolinadeivid shirt and rubbed his hairy chest. He picked up the wine bottle and a rose and ran slowly upstairs dancing. The gold necklace swung side to side. Outside the bathroom door he looked at himself and at his Carolinadeivid's briefs and smiled. This is what he was born to do he thought to himself. He placed the rose across his mouth and slowly slid the door open. There she was. She flirtatiously lifted her head and with her index finger she signaled him to come. She looked at him with lust and passion as he walked in his briefs with a rose in his mouth and a wine bottle in his hand. She closed her legs and squeezed. The bathroom was steamy. He placed the wine bottle down and entered the tub slowly. He gave her the rose with his mouth. Mouth to mouth she received the rose and instantly he pulled the rose gently but enough for the pricks to cut her tongue. She took the rose and dropped it onto the floor. He looked at her as blood droplets trickled down the ridges of her lips and onto her chin. He looked at her gray eyes with lust and passion. He leaned closer and closer and licked up the blood before kissing her passionately sucking her lips. She sighed with passion and clipped his back with her legs.

She looked at him and whispered in his ears.

"I longed for you."

"Really? I thought you wanted to kill me," he whispered kissing her lips gently.

She stubbed him with all her tongue and they snogged passionately. She looked at him with these beautiful gray eyes.

"Thought we make love first."

"Love don't kill."

She smiled flirtatiously.

"Who said I am in love with you?"

"Let's just say that you are not that good at concealing your feelings."

They made passionate love in the tub. They changed positions. Delta sat in the tub and she sat on him. He squeezed both her arms. Her hair covered his face before she slumped on top of him.

"Funny I used to read your mails."

"What mails?"

"All your calls for help. All your lusts and wishes."

"Really. Did God send you? He is the only one who knows my wishes."

Delta smiled and kissed her all over caressing her body.

"I am your wish number 10."

She sat up straight and looked at him.

"Who sent you?"

Delta touched her lips and pushed her long hair sideways sensually.

"God makes all our wishes come true."

She kept quiet for a while.

"Really?"

He nodded his head.

"So, does that mean...?"

She didn't even finish talking before he replied.

"Yes."

She quickly checked for something inside the tub.

Delta smiled and placed his arm on her neck.

"Where is my gun?"

He laughed gently and looked outside the tub and lifted the gun. She laughed sarcastically.

"But you said that I have to fulfill my wishes?"

"Hmm that's correct."

"So, give me the gun."

Delta placed the gun down outside the tub.

"Where is he I know he is watching or listening somewhere right here?" asked Delta.

"I don't know what you are talking about."

"Let me guess he likes to watch you fuck?"

She smiled seductively getting up.

"Ah, I see. You like him to watch you fuck."

She knelt and took the gun and pointed it at Delta. She waved at him asking him to move out of the bathroom. He walked out of the bathroom and headed to the bedroom. They entered the bedroom and instantly she placed the gun on his forehead. He grabbed her hair and pulled. She cocked up the gun. He walked to the bed. She pushed him onto the bed and sat on him. She looked at the mirror above the ceiling. She raised the gun and fired a shot. Delta instinctively pushed her aside then he rolled sideways covering his face and off the bed.

"What the fuck are you doing? Oh my God! Be careful not the face."

He instantly got up and looked at himself in the mirror. He had a few small cuts on his forehead and chin and a small amount of blood was running down his forehead.

"What the fuck did you do that for? I said be careful with the face."

He retrieved the gun from her and aimed at her. He slapped her with the outside of his hand. She punched him and then kissed him passionately. He licked the blood on her face. Instantly the door opened wide. Instinctively he pushed her aside and fired a shot. It happened very fast. He looked at her. She was down and in agony. He fired another shot. He staggered backward as well and looked at his shoulder. He clutched the shoulder and then checked his hand for blood. It was covered in blood.

"The bastard shot me!"

He instantly knelt next to Detective Kristy. She had been shot on her side and was bleeding badly. He quickly tried to stop the bleeding.

He got up leaving the gun on the floor. He searched for a cloth to tie her to stop the bleeding. He turned around and instantly a bullet hit him at close range that he jerked backward.

"Ah! What was that for?"

She smiled provocatively and aimed again at him. She growled in pain as she sat up straight leaning against the bed holding her side stomach. She spread open her legs and with the index finger signaled him to come and with the gun she pointed between her legs.

"Let's fuck again before I finish you off."

"Oh! You shot me! I am not supposed to die." shouted Delta kneeling down in front of her.

The cellphone vibrated, and Detective Kristy opened her eyes. She was still in the tub. She looked around and then at herself. She smiled and squeezed the area between her legs.

"Yeah my wish. Delta?"

CHAPTER FIFTEEN

A car parked outside a lab in the city. Detective Braden looked at his watch and tapped at the steering wheel. He wore sunglasses. The car engine's noise cuts through the background music. The song was by Carolinadeivid; Taking Chances. He nodded to the tune of the song. Instantly the passenger door opened. Detective Kristy jumped in.

"Let's go," she advised.

Detective Braden just looked at her before setting off. He changed the radio station. There was the Elinadeivid song Let's Plan Our Future. Detective Kristy smiled. Detective Braden quickly threw a quick glance at her before he changed the radio station. He cursed. He changed the station. A Carolinadeivid song I love you was on air. Detective Kristy looked at him and smiled humming to the tune. Quickly he changed the station.

"Nowadays they play love songs everywhere. Damn it! Who need love at a time like this? You need to stay focused. I am counting on you Partner."

Instantly Detective Kristy looked at him.

"What? What did you say?"

"So, are you telling me that you didn't hear what I said?"

"I was dosing off. Bit tired you know. I wanted today off."

"Don't give me excuses. I want to be sure that I can count on you. Stay focused okay?"

Detective Kristy looked outside the window.

"You are going to get us killed."

"Where are we going?"

Detective Braden didn't reply straight away.

He looked at her.

"Something about you. You look different. Since when you shave your face?"

"What? I don't know what you are talking about."

She smiled.

The detective as far as he can remember had always seen the small blonde mustache on Detective Kristy's face. This day she was smooth. She had shaved the little blonde hairs. Trimmed her eyebrows as well just a bit but enough for him to tell. Detective Braden's heart beat instantly shot up. He quickly steered off the road and harsh brakes to a halt.

"Is it Delta?"

"Leave him out of this."

"Okay."

The detective steered quickly back on the road. He drove very fast like a rally driver. Changing gears even faster. He contacted the headquarters.

"I need a position system on a vehicle."

Delta jumped into his sport convertible car. He sat on the top edge of his seat and wore his shades. He looked around. He noticed that people were ogling him and his car. He smiled before sliding inside the convertible. He drove off quickly. His cellphone rang. It was Eva. He harsh brakes in the middle of the road before making a U-turn. The car soon sped off. Delta's car overtook Detective Braden's car at a fast speed.

"What the fuck?"

Detective Kristy smiled.

"What are you smiling at?"

He looked at the car as it sped off.

"Speaking of the devil. Fasten your seat belt."

Detective Kristy smiled and looked outside the car. The engine noise made by Delta's car was heard even after the car had passed.

"He can't drive like that!"

Detective Kristy did not say anything she just looked at Detective Braden.

"I bet he has a lady in that car."

He looked at Detective Kristy. This time she didn't smile she checked and made sure that she had fastened well her seat belt.

"Yes, I got your attention, huh?"

Delta looked in the rear-view mirror before he cursed.

"Damn it!"

He quickly dialed Eva.

"Pick up. Pick up."

He whispered.

He pressed the gas pedal down as he heard the siren sound getting louder and louder.

"What does he want now?"

He opened the glove compartment and looked for his gun. He checked the glove near the car gears and saw his gun. He closed the lid of the glove compartment and looked in the rear-view mirror. He looked again and cursed.

"Both?"

He started indicating to stop on the side of the road. Detective Kristy looked in the rear-view mirror to check how she looked. Instantly the detective's cellphone started ringing. The two cops threw each other a quick glance. Detective Kristy looked at Detective Braden's cellphone and saw who the call was from. Detective Braden looked at her with deep hooded evil eyes. Instantly she felt a sharp pain in her heart. She instantly looked at Delta's car. Delta was pulling off on the side of the road. Instantly her cellphone started ringing too. She looked at the cellphone screen and then at Detective Braden. She answered the phone without saying anything and listened attentively.

She dropped the cellphone and gazed at Delta.

It was like a dream. She felt like she was having a nightmare. She froze for a while. She saw as if in slow motion the opening of Delta's car door. She saw him got out his head first and then the leg out. His volumized yet short hair dangling. He got out and looked at the car behind. Detective Kristy looked at Detective Braden as he checked his gun. They both heard a crackling voice and a voice talking and calling Detective Kristy's name. She looked between her legs and saw the cellphone. She in slow motion pushed the cellphone to the floor of the car. She looked at Detective Braden as he stepped out of the car. She looked in front and saw Delta looking back in his car. He then swiftly looked at her. He smiled and took off his sunglasses. Their eyes met. She instantly pulled out her gun and swung open the car door so fast that it caught Delta's attention. He stopped and looked at them his face trembling with rage. She got out leaning on the door before aiming at him. Detective Braden was now walking toward him. Delta saw Detective Kristy aiming the gun at him. He quickly jumped back into the car and drove off skidding and sending smoke into the air.

"Damn it! What are you doing? I had him. Get in! Get in!"

Delta cursed repeatedly raving the car. He drove like he had never done before. He cursed and quickly checked his gun. He kept looking in the rear-view mirror his face shaking and in disbelief.

"I should have killed him!"

Delta got the gun and placed it between his legs. The next time he looked in the rear-view mirror he saw the car approaching at a fast speed. He held the steering wheel firm. He skidded the car around the corner steering fast to correct the skid. He changed gears quickly. Still cursing. Detective Kristy put her head outside the car and fired a shot.

Detective Braden looked at her with eyes that seemed to ask what the fuck are you doing warning him?

He pulled his gun.

"Hold this."

Detective Kristy held the steering wheel firmly

He pointed and fired a shot. Delta cursed and ducked for a split second as the side mirror was shattered by a bullet.

Instincts kicked in that he stepped the gas pedal even further. He opened a gap for a while. He looked continuously in the rear-view mirror. Instantly the sound of the ringing of the car phone startled him. He looked at the LCD screen and saw the caller; Eva.

"Damn it."

The car steered out of the road before he parked on the roadside. He ran into the building in the city. The detective's car parked behind a few minutes later. Detective Braden leading, entered the building signaling. Stealthily they entered the building checking everywhere. Detective Braden signaled Detective Kristy to go the other direction, but she stopped and followed him instead. She checked the doors of the offices. Most of the doors were shut and locked except one. She signaled to Detective Braden. The cops stealthily entered looking everywhere.

"Come out now I know you are in here!"

Shouted Detective Braden.

The cops looked at each other.

"Why are you trying to kill me?"

The cops looked at each other.

Detective Braden signaled to Detective Kristy.

Detective Kristy went the other way.

"Come out! You will be safe. We don't want to hurt you."

"What the fuck you want? Why are you shooting at me?"

"Come out we want to talk!"

"Okay but don't shoot. Okay?"

Delta walked slowly on the open.

"Drop your gun!"

"What the fuck you want?"

"Just talking. Come with us."

He instantly looked around.

"Where is your partner?"

"Detective come out!"

Delta heard noises and when he looked away Detective Braden fired a shot. He jerked backward and dropped the gun. He instantly touched his shoulder.

Detective Braden held firm his gun with both his hands and walked slowly toward Delta. Detective Kristy shouted.

"Don't shoot he has no gun!"

Detective Braden stopped and looked.

"Drop your gun!"

He shouted aiming at Delta.

Delta looked at Detective Braden who raised the gun as if to shoot him in the head.

"No! Not the face."

He looked away.

"What are you doing? He is unarmed! He has no gun."

Detective Braden stopped and lowered his gun. Detective Kristy placed her gun down and looked at Delta who was covering his face.

"It's okay. He is not going to shoot."

Delta looked at Detective Braden. Detective Kristy looked at Delta. His face said it all. She instinctively turned around. Detective Braden pulled the trigger. Delta slumped on one knee in front of Detective Kristy.

"He has no gun! Don't shoot!"

Screamed Detective Kristy body-guarding Delta. She looked at Detective Braden raising her hand. She instantly saw him jerk backward at the same time she heard shots being fired. She turned around and looked at Delta. He was holding a gun which he had pulled from his back. She instinctively threw a quick glance at the gun on the ground. She ducked and picked up the gun and rolled before kneeling in front of him. She pointed a gun at him. He pointed back.

"Why are you trying to kill me?"

"I am not trying to kill you."

"The second time now you aimed at me!"

She instantly lowered her gun. Looking at him.

"Okay! Okay! I was not trying to kill you."

"Don't lie to me! I saw you. You got out of the car and aimed at me."

"He was going to kill you."

"He didn't aim at me. He was coming to talk."

"No. It's not what it seems."

Delta started shaking with rage.

"You upset me by lying!"

"I will never hurt you. Delta. You escaped, didn't you?" She smiled and looked at him. He could see her gray eyes glittering and shining. She smiled. He felt the smile. It was genuine. He lowered his gun and instantly she growled in pain. He grabbed her in his arms as she fell.

He looked at her. She looked at her stomach and searched for blood. She looked in her bloodied hand. She looked at Delta. She did not even bother checking who had blasted her at close range. She slumped in Delta's arms. She looked at him and smiled.

"You are very handsome."

Delta looked in front of him.

He looked back at her.

"Shh don't talk. You will be alright."

"Delta? I protected you, didn't I?"

Delta cried holding her in his arms.

"I swear I will never hurt you."

She smiled.

"He was going to shoot you. He could have killed you. I frightened you, so you run away."

A tear ran down one of her eyes.

"You touched me. I am not afraid to die. I saved you. God will save me."

She paused and creased her face in agony for a while touching the side of her stomach.

"I nearly killed you? Remember the first time we met?"

She smiled and touched his face.

"I nearly run you over. I could have killed you."

"Shh."

"Ever since that day I swore I will protect you. Make up for that day."

She smiled and touched his lips. She closed her eyes and protracted her lips.

Delta slowly leaned toward her and kissed her passionately.

She smiled then coughed and wiped blood coming from her mouth.

"I saved you. I am not an angel, but I saved you. You might not believe me, but they gave us an order to kill you. I just couldn't. I love you."

She closed her eyes and lifted her lips.

"You go to hell!"

"No! No! No! Don't shoot."

A bullet sound pierced the air at the same time a man's cry tore the otherwise silent atmosphere.

A spot car revved around a corner. Inside was Delta and Eva. He looked at her.

"What took you so long? She could have shot me."

Eva looked at him speechless.

"Now you can't talk?"

"I was crying."

Instantly Delta screeched the car to a halt.

"What? Why?"

Eva did not say anything.

"Why were you crying?"

Eva opened the door before storming out of the car. She ran for a while sobbing.

He chased after her.

"Hold on! Wait there. Where do you think you are going?"

He caught up with her and hugged her tightly. She slapped him. He held her before she broke down crying.

"Tell me what's wrong."

"You just want the money?"

"What do you mean?"

She sobbed profusely.

"You are like a machine. Why did you not stop me?"

"I am lost."

"You will never find someone like her. Someone who love you that way. You should have believed her and stopped me from shooting her."

She paused while sobbing.

"I think you shot my mum too."

"Don't say that."

"If someone loves you that way why would you not change? I think you shot my mum just like you let me shoot her."

"Don't start. This is my job. It's either I do the job, or someone else is going to come after me. This is the only way I can save you."

"Killing people, you love."

"It's my job."

Eva sobbed uncontrollably. Delta hugged her.

She looked at him before touching his heart.

"Are you sure you have my father's heart? Sometimes I think it's good this way that I never met him. What I don't understand is that if you have my father's heart why don't you feel at all? Does that mean he was a monster?"

"I don't feel like your father. I have a mind of my own. I understand your father was a good man."

They sat down for a while.

"Does that mean that Kristy was on your list?"

Delta did not say anything. He looked at her. He sighed and covered his face with his hands.

"Let me see the list."

Delta took off his shirt. He lifted his arm and showed her the list on his rib-cage.

She looked and read the names.

"All this list?"

She looked down the list and instinctively stared at him with haunted eyes. She pushed him to the ground before running for it. She entered the car and instinctively reversed before making a U-turn and driving away.

"Hey! What do you think you are doing! Come back

here!" shouted Delta chasing after the car.

He threw his shirt in the direction the car went before kneeling.

He looked at the list all the way down. There were two names at the bottom tattooed in Russian language.

He got his phone and translated the last two.

"Ewalinka Volkov. Eva!"

A huge screamed tore the skies.

"It's a long list. Where is the Underwear-model?"

CHAPTER SIXTEEN

A car parked outside the cemetery. The man wearing glasses and dark clothes remained inside the car. Far away was a funeral ceremony. People had gathered around and were burying Detective Kristy. The man sat in the car sobbing softly. He got out of his car and stood a few feet from his car and watched the ceremony from a distance. The coffin started lowering down slowly. The man stood still on attention and saluted.

"Yes, Officer safe journey!"

A tear trickled down one of his eyes and landed on his polished shoe.

He quickly ran to his car and entered inside. The priest caught his attention so as everyone that they all stopped what they were doing and looked at him. He quickly made a U-turn and drove as fast as he can out of the cemetery until he joined the main road. A huge cloud of dust rose into the sky.

"Ewalinka!"

A car slowly came to a halt outside a house in one of the suburbs. Leah the Underwear-model got out of the car. She stopped and looked around. She checked her gun and attached the camera first. Then the silencer. All this time in lingerie and wearing an open, long jacket-like dress. She slowly fastened the jacket buttons until it was a complete dress. She shoved the gun in the pocket and walked in high heels to the house.

She broke into the house. Stealthily she tip-toed in the house going through the lounge. She was about to leave the lounge going up the steps to the bedroom when a calm voice startled her.

"Underwear-model where do you think you are going?"

She stopped and smiled. Very calmly she replied.

"You are everywhere. I am just surprised to see you here."

"I was thinking the same thing."

"I heard you messed up again."

"They assigned you?"

"You know the drill. You mess up someone follows."

"Protocol, huh?"

There was a moment of silence.

"So, what are you doing here? You came for your left overs?"

Delta breathed heavily.

"Let's just say we are related and don't ask me how because I can't explain."

"They never assign you to kill your own child."

"What do you know?"

"I am going in to finish her off."

"Trust me, we are related. I got her father's heart. You know...?"

There was a moment of silence.

"I guess no modeling for you tonight. I am taking her to Russia with me. I am out."

"Nonsense. They will still come after you and her."

"I will take my chances. I lost someone today."

"Oh Delta. I can't miss. I must have a clean sheet you know that."

"I promise I will be indebted to you forever."

"Russia, huh?"

"Nearly twenty years now in the wilderness. You reach a time when you just can't go on. I loved this woman."

Leah sat down and sighed.

"Why didn't you save her?"

"Just playing stupid you know."

There was a moment of silence.

"That explains why you took so long. I knew it. We had a bet you would take her out the first day that day on the road."

"I know that was the plan."

"So, you fall in love?"

Delta smiled and sat down.

"The moment I looked into her eyes. I just knew it. It was like let's plan our future right now."

"Should have opted out."

"Trust me, I tried but Eva?"

"They had already sent my replacement. Just like they have already sent hers; you."

"Are we ever going to settle down like everyone else? I am longing for love. I don't think I can go another day."

"I think they have plans for you."

Delta and Leah threw each other a quick glance.

"Ooh no. I don't want that burden."

"By the way things are going. I think you are the chosen one. Sacrifice makes you stronger. That pain, all these years in the wilderness, all makes you determined. Pain is a weapon they know that very well."

Delta moved closer to Leah.

"Let me see if you can relieve my pain."

He kissed her passionately.

"I am ready for you babe."

Leah flashed her sexy lingerie flirtatiously.

"We can't do it here. If she wakes up, I am dead meat. You know the drill."

"Don't be afraid. She is not jealous of me."

Leah looked confused.

"Excuse me. But she whacked Kristy when she kissed you If I heard correctly."

Delta sighed.

"Kristy was a dirty cop. She whacked several unarmed couples with Braden the early days. I was specifically assigned to do her. If you know what I mean. They want a new start. A complete fresh start."

"So, are you saying that her love for you was a fake?"

Leah sat up straight.

"Fear."

"Did she know that you were sent to kill her?"

Delta sighed for a while.

"Staged from day one to put her in that state of mind. Fear induced by the fact that she nearly run me over. After that, that incident plays a major role in her decision making. She soon starts thinking about me all day long and before you know it she is in love with me. That state makes her weak in every sense. The sex; out of this world. After that she will do anything for me."

"You mean die for you?"

"Literally take bullets for me."

"I told you before that charm can kill but you didn't believe me."

They both laughed softly.

Leah stopped and looked toward the bedroom door.

"Ewalinka?"

"Hmm!"

Delta laughed sarcastically.

"What is it?"

"Can you believe it that she has my father's heart?"

"No way. You have her father's heart?"

Delta nodded.

"You understand why I have to kill all these evil fucks?"

"Are you saying that they removed normal hearts so that they experiment on both of you?"

Delta kept quiet and started breathing heavily.

"Do you know how confusing this is? I look at her and feel like I am with my father? Who on earth would do something like this?"

"So, the President is right. We have to kill all?"

"They harvested body parts extensively and played games with people's lives. Imagine someone who removes an otherwise perfect heart for a transplanted one where the donor had suffered a violent death?"

"The trauma I think is unbearable."

"To make things worse, they replaced normal hearts with a heart of a person who died a violent death. At times I feel that pain."

Delta clenched his fists. He got up and sobbed.

"You see why I am determined to kill all these evils." Leah stood up and followed him. She grabbed him.

"I will make you feel good. Come."

She grabbed his hand and pulled him onto the couch. She opened her jacket dress. She took off her underwear and kissed him passionately.

"Come fuck me. Come."

She whispered.

Delta was about to when a shadow suddenly appeared on the steps to the bedroom.

Delta looked at Ewalinka and then at Leah.

"I might have your father's heart, but I have my own mind, my own feelings and thoughts okay. You can't fuck her in front of me."

"It's okay don't shoot."

Leah looked at Ewalinka and then at Delta. She looked haunted as if she had seen a ghost.

"What is it Leah?" asked Delta.

"Am I on your list?"

Delta looked shocked and scared.

"That can't be right."

He quickly switched on the light and looked at the last name.

"Is this your name?"

She did not reply she looked at Ewalinka.

"Don't shoot."

"She is on your list. She is on my list too." Ewalinka stretched her hand to reveal a tattoo with names of people. They both looked at the list. Delta and Ewalinka both looked at Leah.

"Where is your list?"

They asked at the same time.

Leah remained silent.

Ewalinka cocked up the gun.

"I said don't shoot!"

Leah lifted her groin area. Delta held her buttocks and raised them to look at the tattoo on her pubic region.

"Why didn't you get the tattoo done somewhere where there is more space, like your butt."

They all laughed.

"Very funny, are you saying that my butt is big?"

Ewalinka leaned to see as well.

"Eww! What are you doing? I don't want to be looking at this at the same time with you." said Delta jokingly.

"What? Maybe my name is there too. I have to see it for myself before I put a bullet in her heart."

"Hey no one talked about shooting each other."

Delta and Ewalinka threw each other a quick glance.

Ewalinka aimed to shoot.

"What did I say?"

"If we don't shoot her she is just going to shoot us all?"

Delta stood up.

"Why would they want us to kill each other?"

Leah looked at Delta.

"What did you do? Were you a cop before?"

"No."

"What about you?"

"No, I was a lingerie model."

"What about you?"

They all looked at Ewalinka.

"I was his father?"

She said that pointing at Delta.

They all laughed.

"My father was a politician."

"Wait, a minute. We have to go to France or Russia.?"

Ewalinka got really upset.

"See you are always on the run. Let's stick together and finish the job that way they will never come for us."

Delta walked in the lounge.

"They are letting the cleaners clean themselves."

"What?"

"We have reached the last stages. Look you two are the last names on my list. After a few killings then technically, we will start shooting each other."

"They must kill all us too. No evidence and no one will talk. A real clean start."

"Bastards!"

They all sat down speechless.

"I guess that makes sense."

Delta looked at Ewalinka and pointed toward the bedroom. He looked at Leah.

"Damn we are going to die. Let me see that tattoo again. Leah lifted her groin.

"Father?"

Shouted Delta sarcastically looking at Ewalinka.

"Stop calling me your father. I am not."

They all laughed.

Ewalinka slammed the bedroom door as she entered the bedroom.

Leah looked at Delta.

"You want to see the list? What list? You think I don't know what you want?"

They both laughed as Delta and Leah played cat and mouse.

"On a serious note. Will you come with me to Russia?"

Instantly the bedroom door opened.

"Will you come with us to USA? Russia? Russia? What Russia? I told you I want to be an Underwear-model?"

"Thank God we have Leah here she will help you with that."

"So why you are saying Russia. Super models only in USA!"

"Father! Can't you see I am busy."

Shouted Delta jokingly.

Ewalinka pointed a gun at Delta.

"Call me father one more time and I will shoot you."

She slammed the door closed.

They started laughing.

"Father!"

He jokingly shouted trying to annoy Ewalinka.

"I heard you!"

She shouted.

I guess we must go to the USA.

Instantly the door opened.

Ewalinka started walking like a model on the catwalk. They both sat down and looked at her. They started clapping hands and applauding.

"I have never seen you this happy before," said Delta.

"You are now starting to sound like my real father," replied Eva.

Delta and Leah looked at each other and smiled.

"What's funny?" asked Eva

They both started laughing.

"I wish I can say the same way."

"Son, you deserve some beatings," shouted Ewalinka

getting a pillow and hitting Delta and Leah with it. The three played cat and mouse.

"Dad are you sure we are going to the USA?"

They both looked at each other.

"She called me dad!"

whispered Delta.

Delta's face shone with happiness.

"Yes dad."

"Darling can you answer your daughter. Are we going to the USA? Yes or no?"

Delta hugged both the two women in his life.

"Off course my daughter and my beautiful wife-to-be."

"USA here we come!"

They shouted at the same time.

CHAPTER SEVENTEEN

Later that evening they were watching the television.

The President was addressing the nation.

"This is just the beginning. We pray and hope that everyone will cooperate and make this project an easy one to implement. We are hoping that everyone will cooperate and abide by Directive 17. Surely, we don't want to go to war. We have cleaned all evil. We hope that everyone here strongly believes in our project and want to work with us. For those who think they are above the law, take my word for it. You shall feel the full force of Directive 17. There shall be no mercy. It's either you are with us or against us. It's going to be hard, but change doesn't come cheap, but we are well prepared to deal with it. I hope that you are all ready."

He paused for a while.

"Tomorrow's World Order shall see the plans through until the world has established an effective body that will deal with today's global problems. Today's leaders have backtracked taking us back to the medieval times. The whole system has gone bonkers relying on digital-man-made agents to function properly. We still spend $ trillions globally making weapons. Sometimes war is the answer. A new beginning. Destruction of the things we don't need; weapons. Ladies and gentlemen above all this, this gives me the President, the chance to play God and eliminate all evil once and for all. Uphold the rule of the law. Surely you don't want to be on my *To-do-list* or you will feel the full force of Directive 17. I pray that we will never implement Directive 17 that means everyone changing for the better. We shall aim to be superior humans as nature intended. Change or we will change you or eliminate you. Thank You."

"Ladies and gentlemen the President."

Miles away.

Nick got up and sat down.

"You see? Not everything is bad after all. Sometimes we must do evil to establish good forever."

"What are you saying? Start making sense."

"You mean you killed a kid to save me?"

Gabriel stood there looking at Nick. He briefly smiled.

"Do you know that they use kids to wipe out the entire generation?"

"A kid died for nothing. Surely there is a way to solve this?"

Gabriel laughed.

"You have to change your thinking otherwise you will never win."

"Gabriel don't tell me these kid-soldiers are real?"

Instantly Nick jumped up and touched his forehead.

"Ouch what just happened to me?"

Gabriel laughed.

"A minute ago, you said there must be a way. So, tell me how we can solve this?"

"Fight to the end like soldiers."

Gabriel laughed and walked to the window.

"Fight like soldiers. Huh?"

He laughed and puffed his electrical cigarette.

"Mr. Nick do you mean with guns.?"

"Of course. This is a war. How else can you fight?"

"That's the reason all have failed."

Gabriel took a gun and threw it next to Nick.

"You said if you know who is doing that you will kill him. Right?"

"Absolutely blast the motherfucker at point-blank."

Gabriel got up and open his drawer and gave a gadget to Nick.

"Just take a lift and follow the directions to the floors above."

Nick stood up about to leave.

"By the way you will need a gun."

Gabriel pointed at the gun on the sofa.

Nick looked upset.

"You are telling me that the person doing this to me is here?"

"He is the agent working on commission. The real person I guess you have to figure it out yourself."

Nick quickly grabbed the gun. He looked at the gadget in his hand the dots where moving very fast.

"You will lose the trail. Hurry!"

Nick left the office and quickly pressed the buttons of the lifts. He saw the dots on the gadgets moving very fast. He took the steps and ran as fast as he can to the top levels. He held his gun firmly. He looked at the gadget and followed the signal. He quickly leaned against a door and listened. Instantly the movements stopped. His heart beat rose instantly. He held his gun firmly and waited. He turned and pushed the door hard. Inside was a kid maybe ten years old with a joy stick in his hand. The boy as soon as he had seen him. He moved the joystick and laughed. Nick felt like his head was being turned around. He aimed the gun.

"Drop that down now."

"I can't until you are dead."

Nick stopped and pretended to have been shot as he slumped to the ground.

The kid then pulled a gun from his back and aimed at Nick.

"No! Stop! Put the gun down."

"I don't miss. They killed Billy?"

"Who is Billy? Who killed Billy?"

The kid pointed in the other room.

"Okay maybe he is still alive. Can I check him maybe he needs a doctor fast okay?"

The kid looked at Nick.

"I might help him for sure."

"Are you sure you can help him?"

The kid instantly put the gun down.

"Come quickly take him to the hospital."

Nick ran in the other room.

A boy the same age was in a pool of blood. Blasted at close range.

Instantly Nick stopped and touched his chest.

"What's wrong? Is he dead? If you can't save him, then maybe I have to blast you too."

Nick did not say anything. He just stood there speechless. He only woke up from the nightmare when he heard the clicking of the gun.

He knelt and felt the boys' pulse.

He felt a bullet shattering his flesh.

He remembered Californika injecting a very warm bullet into his flesh. He thought about Angela too. He briefly smiled when he thought about Karolina. He squinted his eyes and touched his head. He knew that he will never see her again and his kid. This is the part he disliked about this job. He had done the same a few years back. Start a family only to have disappeared and being pronounced dead a few years later. He sat there and looked at the boy's lifeless body. He remembered Gabriel telling him that he had subjugated to one of them. He never thought it to be a boy. He felt a cold shiver down his spine. Surely that could have been my boy. He thought. He looked at the other boy. He saw a tear drop from only one eye. In slow motion he followed it all the way until it hit the ground. He put his gun down.

"He saved me. Bloody cowards! They use you, kids.

The whole system is corrupt. What are you fighting for?"

"It's a war. Soldiers die. He was just unlucky. I have seen this before."

"How old are you? Maybe ten? What do you know about war?"

"That's what they all say until I put a bullet in their brain then they start taking me seriously. Give me your gun!"

Nick smiled and pushed the gun to the boy.

"I am not going to run," replied Nick.

The boy looked upset.

"No. It's not that you can run. You can't run!"

Nick looked surprised and scanned the area.

"How is that so?"

Instantly a beep sound caught his attention. The boy smiled and placed the gun down.

"What's funny."

"They just finished triangulating. You can't run now. He is now your bobby trap. He took your bullet we will reverse everything. Right now, he is in an idle state, paused, just like you yesterday after they shot you. You die too."

"There is no need for anyone to die."

"They can raise him if I find someone to subjudicate

to and you are the perfect one. Nick instantly got up. He knew the boy was telling the truth. His heart tore apart. He instantly remembered Gabriel's words.

"Blast him at close range."

He instantly looked at the gun. The boy quickly took the gun but threw it on the couch further away.

"You don't believe me. Go and get the gun."

The boy pointed at him with the other gun.

He looked at the dead boy first and then at the gun. To get the gun, he had to pass the dead boy's body. He also remembered Gabriel telling him not to pass the boy twice. He stopped and looked at the dead boy again. He instantly turned and walked away going out.

"I am going to shoot you anyway."

Instantly he stopped and saw the boy pointing the gun at him.

"Walk past him and give him his life back get a gun and I will shoot you so only you die. He will wake up. They didn't tell you what to do?" asked the boy.

"Who are you talking about? Who is they?"

The boy pointed at the ceiling.

"They have camera's everywhere? They watch you?"

"They are very bad. They use electricity to torture us if we refuse."

"So, what did they tell you?"

"They told me that I was to go and play with Billy today."

"What. I thought you said he died……"

Nick stopped for a while thinking.

"Is that Billy?"

He pointed at the dead boy.

He remembered Gabriel talking to him. He remembered how enraged he was. He realized that he did not do what everyone expected. He was to blast this boy. He walked toward the boy and as soon as he passed the boy he felt like someone has tripped him somehow that he felt all his energies escaping. He fell like a lifeless doll hitting his head very hard on the floor that he blacked out.

Days Later

Gabriel watched Nick sleeping in the hotel. His eyes were moving very fast beneath closed eyelids. A woman entered the hotel. Nick could smell the fragrances of her perfume. He instantly smiled and instantly his eyelids snapped open. He looked around. Everything appeared blurred. He rubbed his eyes and saw Andrea. She walked toward him wearing a small bikini and high heels. He tried thinking what had happened.

"Where am I?"

Instantly Gabriel got up and replied

"In a hotel somewhere nice and beautiful."

"Where is the boy?"

"What boy? One of your dreams?"

He looked at his chest and felt the bullet entry point. Instantly he sat up and looked around. Gabriel looked at Andrea and instantly she took off her knickers and bra and started touching Nick.

"Wait! Gabriel tell me where the boy is?"

"You know the job. We talked about this."

"What do you mean? I said where is the boy?"

Gabriel walked to the table in the hotel and lifted a wine glass. He looked at Andrea. She started touching him all over.

"You said you wanted to see your son."

"Yes, when I finished this job. Definitely, I would not want anything to do with you or this job. Time to spend time with my son."

Gabriel got very angry.

"You don't get it do you? I told you it's just a vacation. Do you make babies on vacation? Now see you let me clean up your mess."

Nick felt a lump choking his throat. He had never felt such a rage before.

"Are you saying… aah …no, no!"

He cried profusely.

"Andrea, here make another one. That boy saved you with his own life."

Nick pushed Andrea aside and got up.

"Was that my boy?"

"You said you wanted to meet your son. That was your son. Move on. Make another, Andrea is here ready for you."

Nick punched Gabriel very hard.

"You bastard surely I am going to kill you,"

He sobbed. Andrea came closer and started touching him.

"Why my boy?"

Gabriel punched Nick back.

"Listen. What can I do with your son? I invested millions on this project. I have no use of kids. I would rather kill all your kids if that means saving you."

"Who was the other kid? Where is he?"

Gabriel looked at Nick.

"You didn't know?"

"Know what?"

"That's your son too."

Nick kept quiet.

"Billy is my son? I meant the other boy same age."

Gabriel looked at Andrea. She instantly walked to the

table and retrieved photos.

"Do you know this woman?"

Nick looked at the photos.

Yes sure.

"Why are you asking me?"

Nick looked at Gabriel and then Andrea.

"Nicoleta!"

"So, you know? See you are leaving trails everywhere. Assassins can't have a family. She said that you slept with her. You wanted a baby girl. When she found out that the baby was a boy she didn't tell because you wanted a girl."

"I have a son. Where is he?"

He looked very excited but instantly felt saddened.

"I have two sons'? Oh Billy!"

He sobbed profusely.

"Where is my son?"

"You think it's only them? Karolina had twins. All boys."

"What? Twins."

Instantly his face changed.

"I swear you kill my boys I am going to kill you."

"You know the drill. I have to clean all your mess."

Nick lunged at Gabriel.

"Damn it! You blood evil monster! They are my boys. You can't touch them."

Gabriel walked toward the window.

"You had them when you were assigned to me. Therefore, my property and like I said I don't use and don't need kids. You know the drill I have to clean all your mess."

"I swear I will kill you!"

Nick shook with rage.

"Andrea is here. A new start. You are out as of today. New passport new identity. Andrea will give you a girl. You never cared about your sons anywhere."

"You know me now?"

"You never asked or ran away to go and see them."

"Because I know they will kill them too. Look, they use kid-soldiers. The whole system relies on kid-soldiers. What divine calling? All these tattoos, all tricks to separate the kids from their parents."

"I knew you would not shoot the boy. They had set you up so that you kill your own son."

"So where is the other boy? My son?"

Gabriel looked at him.

"But you said you want a beautiful daughter so what are you waiting for she is ovulating, and time is ticking."

"Excuse us then."

"You would prefer them to watch you and hear everything than me?"

"I will kill all. World a better place without such evil."

Gabriel heard several gunshots sounds through his headphones and smiled. He sipped his wine.

"That's my son."

"What?" asked Andrea doing some nude yoga.

He smiled.

"Aah" she screamed passionately.

"What I don't understand is that why you scream so passionately when it's just yoga?"

"It's not just yoga. It's called nude yoga."

They both laughed.

"Hurry up, he will wait for you at the airport."

"Russia?"

"Romania."

"Salut ce mai faci,"

"Bine."

A car parked outside a house.

Nicoleta walked to the window and looked outside. Instantly she felt something. Her heart paced fast. She ran down the stairs and outside the yard. She stood outside the gate and looked.

"Nick!"

She looked back and shouted.

"Kyson! Kyson! Daddy is here!"

A door opened, and all the people looked at the woman smartly dressed up in a suit. She walked straight with a raised chin. Everyone stood up and welcomed her. The conference hall was all packed up. There were news reporters all over everyone scrambling to be in front. The woman raised her hands and there was instant silence.

"For the past years we have sent people all over the world. The results are starting to come in. I must admit, it was a long and painful process. You must agree with me that sometimes it's not easy to point fingers and accuse people of crimes against humanity. We have looked at all the cases. I think there are very good reasons to believe that we might need to implement and enforce Directive 17."

She paused as everyone looked and listened very attentively.

"Looking at a large scale I think there are strong grounds to believe that some of us have fallen below standard to such an extent that their acts amount to crimes against humanity. Mind you, you must view all the arguments presented with this in mind that we are in the 21st century. A century or two ago some acts might have been regarded as normal. We expect everyone to move with the times. What was correct a few years ago cannot be okay today and having that in mind? I think no matter what. Crimes against humanity must be taken seriously no matter who the offender is. This issue is aggravated by the fact that there is no effective body with powers and jurisdiction to bring the most offenders to Hague but let me stress this out. That does not mean the world can't act. Where there is no proper body to bring complacent and arrogant perpetrators to justice as a global movement we can initiate and implement Directives against countries concerned. Crimes against humanity are global issues that require a global solution. We will vote. All countries are to present their grievances against others. We will look at all the cases. If most people vote in favor of the implementation of the Directive, we will nominate a task force and proceed with swiftness and ruthlessness. We all agree that people's beliefs change with time and in this era, we cannot tolerate any forms of torture, no matter for what reason. Torture must never be tolerated or justified as it has very bad connotations. We must not tolerate, encourage or permit the manufacture of weapons of mass destruction [WMD] or their equivalent Remotely Operated Evil Implemented Medical Devices [ROEIMD] and the information we have and looking at all the previous epidemics, we have strong reasons that most of the crimes fall in this category. All world governing bodies like the World Medical Association prohibits the making and implantation of devices namely ROEIMDs that can be used as lethal high voltage emitting torturing devices. We can no longer accept weapons manufacture with intent to use them to rob others of their resources. We can no longer accept the production of lethal strains of all kinds of agents be it digital, biotechnological or any forms. We cannot let others backtrack taking us back to the times when we had no rights at all. We say change with everyone else or we will change you. Global problems require global solutions."

She paused.

"I know some will accuse us of adopting socialist policies again. I think it's fair that everyone acts fairly. Where someone plays God, we will not hesitate to propose and implement with swiftness a global package. I mean every country participating in the attack from all angles. We don't want war but sometimes war is the answer. Some people only open their eyes when they are being attacked. They will take everyone seriously then. All we are asking is for everyone to cooperate and uphold global laws. Having that in mind. I would like to introduce you to Tomorrow's World Order [TWO]. The overseer if you like as all current institutions can't address global issues. Ladies and Gentlemen, I present the honorable President of Tomorrow's World Order Mr. David...." The crowd started applauding and looking around.   THE END